HA'PENNY TOP AND FARTHING TAIL

by

BETTE VICKERS

as serialised by
BBC Radio Humberside

HUTTON PRESS
1986

Hutton Press Ltd.
130 Canada Drive, Cherry Burton, Beverley
North Humberside, HU17 7SB

Printed by Clifford Ward & Co.
(Bridlington) Ltd.
55 West Street, Bridlington, East Yorkshire
YO15 3DZ

ISBN 0 907033 38 5

To Charles and Dae
who made it all possible

FOREWORD

Bridlington, at the end of the First World, is the setting for this third book based on her family by author Bette Vickers.

"Fed Up To Top Attic" and "Life's Golden Time" introduced us to the main characters of Thom and Esther, Wilf and Ada. In "Ha'penny Top and Farthing Tail" Wilf is now dead, killed in the War, and Ada is trying to come to terms with her loss and bring some normality back to her life. She starts up her own business with her sister Aggie and all goes well until Rob comes on the scene. The love of Rob by both sisters divides the family, and it remains divided until the christening of Ada and Rob's daughter many years later.

Those who have enjoyed listening to the BBC Radio Humberside serials "Fed Up To Top Attic" and "Ha'penny Top and Farthing Tail" or those who have read the first two books will delight in renewing their acquaintance with the characters. And those coming to read of this family for the first time will soon be caught up in their happiness and sadness, so well described by Bette Vickers.

The publishers wish to thank Mr. Graham Henderson of BBC Radio Humberside for all his assistance and encouragement in the publication of this book, and John Reveley for the cover design.

CHAPTER ONE

The bells of peace rang throughout the town. Flag-bedecked streets welcomed the heroes home, town dignitaries gave long speeches and spoke of the great debt owed to the men who fought for their country. Ada Tanner took it all in, pursed her lips, but said nothing.

"It's no good saying owt, is it?" she said to herself. "They don't give a damn about me and Wilf, about our plans, and what for I'd like to know. In a year or so not one of 'em will even remember his name."

But she held her tongue for her Mam and Dad's sake. No use in upsetting them, was it? And they were so proud in a sad kind of way — proud of young Stanley — of Wilf and his medal — of George, Isabella's husband, who was being hailed as a right hero and treated like royalty. They even had pride in Alf Appleyard and Harry Tanner and God only knows, if he'd come back, they'd have shunned him like the devil himself. Aye, best to say nowt and let them get on with it.

But she did find it hard to stomach when a gilt-edged invitation arrived asking them all to go to the unveiling of the cenotaph which held every name of the Bridlington lads who had been killed. Even Polly and Gertie were asked, but Alf's name would not be included, with him actually coming from Barnsley.

"By hek. A seat for us all, right at the front. Now that'll be summat to think about," Thom said.

"Well, it's summat I could have done without," Ada snapped. "And I'm damned if I'll go. None of it will bring 'em back, will it?"

Thom frowned and looked across at his wife Esther for help. By hek, Ada didn't half take some dealing with these days.

"Well, it will be a bit of comfort seeing his name engraved, won't it? Something like a grave."

Ada pursed her lips, thinking how many times she had said that she felt nowt like a widow with Wilf not having a grave. 'No known grave,' that's what the official notice said. Ada wanted to know more. She wanted all the details before she could accept that he was really gone. With no known grave he had not been declared dead, only missing believed killed in action.

"It could be a mistake, Mam. This nothingness doesn't feel right. Somebody must have found summat of him," she had said time and time again. When one of the battalion had come home she would go and ask endless questions — had they seen Wilf just before he was supposedly killed? Surely something must have been found. But no, they could tell her nothing. She grieved to see the lads she had known all her life return home shells of men — without limbs, blind, and some in such a state of nerves and shell shock they would never work again.

"Don't you try and tell me owt is worth this bloody lot," she scorned to George and Isabella.

"You try and persuade her to go then, Thom," said Esther. "She listens to you more than anybody else. She should go, you know, if only to reverence Wilf's memory."

"Well, you know what a determined little bugger she is. But aye, you're right lass, she should go."

But when he broached the subject all he got in answer was, "I should have thought you would have acted a bit different to this, Dad. You were never much for the ruddy war as I recall."

"I know, lass, and I still feel the same way. But it's over now. You can't let Wilf down in front of all them folk now, can you? It's not for us I'm asking lass. You know I don't give a damn what folk think. It's Wilf — his memory — that's what I'm on about. What would he think to the way you're carrying on?"

"I'd stop carrying on if somebody could tell me that it hasn't been in vain."

Thom was running out of patience now. "Well, I can't tell you. I don't think God Himself could. But all this carry on won't bring him back. He died a ruddy hero and I reckon you should go and show folk that you're made of the same stuff."

That got home and condescendingly Ada gave in.

"Are you getting owt new, love?" her Mam asked.

Ada knew what that meant. "If you think I'm going to get dressed up in black and wear widow weeds then you've another think coming, 'cos I'm not. I'm going to wear what I wore to get married in. I've got all them marks up and it looks as good as new."

Esther gasped, but kept her peace. At least the lass was going — that was summat.

George arranged to collect them all in the Sewerby carriage. Ada refused, saying she was going down with Polly and Gertie.

"I can't let them go down on their own now, can I, and anyroad I'll feel better stood with the rest of the wives."

6

Every church was represented. The Salvation Army band played and the Mayor unveiled the monument. All very impressive, but it meant nothing to Ada — not until the last moment when they sang the hymn '*O Valiant Hearts.*'

She looked down at the words on the hymn sheet — '*All you had hoped for, all you had you gave,*' and tears welled up. Looking across, she caught her Dad's eye and putting both her arms around Gertie and Polly she sang in a beautifully clear voice that made heads turn to look at this minute figure dressed, not in the expected black, but in dusky pink — an outfit more suited to a wedding. Their faces almost made her giggle through her tears, and she could almost hear Wilf's voice saying, "That's it, short arse — you show 'em."

As the parade broke up she felt a hand on her arm and, turning, she saw Ralph Tinker standing in full dress uniform.

"That's a lovely voice you've got there, Ada. Wilf would have been proud of you."

"No more than I am of him. But tell me this, just tell me this, why the hell would Wilf want to save their Harry — or our George for that matter? It just doesn't make sense."

"War conditions make men do strange things, Ada — things that otherwise they would never have dreamt of doing. It brings out the best in them."

"By killing them, you mean. And nowt could bring out the best in Harry Tanner — he had no best."

"Can I walk you home?" Ralph asked.

She shook her head. "I'm waiting for Gert and Wilf's Mam. They're looking at his name on monument."

"Aren't you going to look as well?"

"Aye, when all rush is over."

He looked down at her hands which clutched a small dried pink carnation. He didn't have to ask what it meant. It was obviously from her wedding bouquet.

"It's for Wilf. It'll make him feel more settled, wherever he is."

"You feel there is something wrong, then?"

She nodded, and then seeing no-one at the cenotaph, walked slowly until she found his name — 'Cpl. J. W. Tanner, M.M.' With trembling fingers she traced the letters cast in bronze and laid her dried flower at the foot of the column. All those years, all those dreams, and this was all it added up to — a name on a cold granite slab.

7

"Come on, Ada, Esther has asked us up for a cup of tea and I'm feeling a bit worn out with all this lot." Polly smiled weakly at her and Ada, pulling herself together, took her arm and walked slowly up the street.

"Try to stop worriting, lass. It can't do any good," were Polly's parting words. But Ada couldn't. It got so bad that she began to have nightmares that woke her up in a sobbing shake, crying out his name. Esther would go into her and try to give some comfort and many a time they would sit out the early hours of the morning in the old kitchen, poking the dying embers of the fire and sipping endless cups of tea.

"You're going to have to accept it, lass, for all our sakes. You're bothering us to death. Wilf would never want this, you know," Esther would say, biting back the words that Ada was still young and might meet someone else.

Surprisingly Polly covered her grief well and at times even she got impatient with Ada. "He's gone, Ada, let him rest. He was my lad after all and if I can take it the least you can do for everybody's sake is to calm yourself down. Look at our Gertie. She's started nursing proper now and is keeping company with another young lad."

Ada's heart finally began to harden with the brusque words and her face set in bitter lines around her mouth. But her plucky spirit won through and gradually she began to pick up the threads of life.

She found that putting all her energy into her work helped and she was rewarded by being made the Manageress's Assistant — a step up, and a position that brought some standing and a lot more brass. Being Ada, however, she still kept her true friends. Others said that power had gone to her head — she had become stuck-up and bossy.

But work had become her salvation and she welcomed the extra overtime. With her earnings and her widow's pension she was nicely off. Each week she deposited a set amount in the Yorkshire Penny Bank. Ralph had offered his services if anything needed sorting out, but she had dismissed this with a curt, "I can sort out what I want, thank you."

"You'll soon be a millionaire. I've never earned money like that in all my days," her Dad would tease her.

But apart from the luxury of buying good quality clothes, Ada spent very little money. If she had any spare time she would go to see Polly or up to Sewerby, but somehow that did not seem the same now. George was not half the man he had been and each step

8

brought back such memories that it was best to let that part of her life fade a bit.

The Whitsun weekend of 1921 was exceptionally busy. The weather was great and it seemed that all the world had decided to forget the war and once more enjoy themselves. The boarding houses were crammed full and this meant that work at the laundry went on late into Saturday. The girls had given a promise to Ada to work until everything was finished, providing they could take Bank Holiday Monday off.

"And if you get through this little lot, you'll deserve it and all," she laughed.

"Why don't you come with us on Monday, Ada. There's a crowd of us going to Filey for the day and then coming back for a fish and chip supper," Lily Hartley asked.

"I don't reckon I'll have much energy left for that," was all Ada made of it.

"For God's sake Ada, you can't go on living with the dead. If Wilf were here he'd be the first to tell you that," Lily snapped. "Anyroad, please yourself." And with that she turned away.

Ada worked through the day thinking on Lily's words. Was she really living with the dead? It was funny she had said that, because during the last few weeks she had sometimes managed to go for two or three days at a time without thinking about Wilf at all. In the rest room she looked at herself in the mirror. God, she looked a sight — a right old woman. Her hair still shone, but her face was tight and lined and there was a permanent frown across her brow. This wasn't the Ada Wilf had loved. Wilf's Ada would have had more gumption than to let herself go like this. Well, she'd show 'em. She'd damn well go on the outing.

Esther was overjoyed when she told her. "About time and all. There's no need to bury your days like this. Get out and enjoy yoursen for a change." Her faced beamed with relief as she spoke.

On Monday morning she stayed in bed until half-past eight, unheard of for Ada, and Esther thought she had changed her mind. But at last she came downstairs all ready dressed to go out.

"I've packed up a bit of grub for you love, and a mite over in case somebody forgets theirs." Trust Mum. She knew some of the lasses would be hard pushed to go on the outing let alone take some grub with them.

9

It was a bright sunny day, but with a nip in the air that brought the colour to her cheeks as she walked to the bus.

Lily greeted her with a shout of glee. "Come on lass. I'm right glad you made the effort. Come on. Put all your worries behind you and let's have a damned good day."

Some had brought coloured streamers and hung them through the open bus windows. They sang as the bus rolled on its way and when they raised their voices in some of the wartime songs, Ada thought she was going to burst out crying, but Lily took hold of her arm and pressed it and soon they were both singing at the tops of their voices.

"I see Billy Acton's come on his own. Has Molly let him off the lead then?" Ada asked Lily.

"I reckon they've fallen out or summat. He's hardly spoken to her all week. I don't know, summat's in the wind."

Ada looked at the common arrogance of Billy Acton. What the hell did the women see in him? But he seemed to attract them like flies. Oh he wasn't bad looking, but a bit too rough for Ada's liking. He'd tried to flirt with her, but she'd soon seen him off with a sharp word in his lug.

They arrived and decided to split up and meet to eat their lunch on the sea front. She'd never been to Filey before and it seemed a nice little place with a surround of green countryside.

"Eh, I never imagined it like this. Just think, it's only about ten miles away and we've never been before."

"Well, let's get a move on or we shan't see it at all," Ada laughed, feeling more in a holiday mood.

Leisurely they strolled along the sea front, had a cup of tea, looked in the shops, bought a souvenir or two, and then reached the end of the street, where they stood looking a little lost. What to do now? From behind a familiar voice called out.

"Oh my God, it's Billy Acton. Come on, let's get a move on." Lily said, but Billy was too quick for them. He moved swiftly to their sides and offered to walk them through the woodland.

"You never know who's around, and I can look after you," he simpered.

"Like hell you can," Lily snapped. "Come on Ada, let's be off."

But to her amazement Ada turned and looked straight at Billy. He wasn't much, but it was a long time since she had gone walking on a man's arm. "It might not be a bad idea to let him go along —

10

just for a walk mind you — nothing more than that," Ada said.

"You do as you like Ada, but I'm off to find the others. Mind you know what you're doing, Ada," Lily warned and turning marched off down the street.

"Well I'm damned. I never thought you'd tek up the offer," Billy laughed. "But you won't regret it I promise you that."

"You're damned right I won't. Come on, let's get going if we are going anywhere."

They set off along the pathway that led to bushes of purple flowering rhododendrons. "Oh, aren't they lovely. Just look at the colours," Ada gasped, and looked at Billy, who up till now had kept a respectable distance.

"They certainly are. Just like you, Ada Skipton." And going to her side he slipped his arms around her waist.

"Tanner, Ada Tanner, if you don't mind. I am — I was married you know," Ada snapped, but made no move to dislodge his arms. Truth was it was nice to feel a man put his arms around her again and to see him looking at you in a special way.

Oh, she'd no thoughts on Billy Acton. No, he wasn't half good enough for her. But it still gave her a nice warm glow inside — a feeling that rather surprised her. "Give us a kiss, Ada. You know I've always fancied you."

He bent his head towards her and at first she held back, and then a wave of emotion passed over her and she let herself be kissed. No-one but Wilf had ever really kissed her and she responded — make-believing for one moment that she was in Wilf's arms again.

"By hell, you're a little fire. I always thought you were, behind that toffee nosed look. Well, I can give you all you want."

He grabbed her and pressed his whole body into her. Again, for a fleeting moment, she responded, pressing herself against the hardness of his body. A rustle from behind the high bank of flowers startled her and she returned back to reality.

"No — no — stop it, Billy — somebody's coming — I don't want this. I've never fancied you — I just lost my bearings for a minute."

She made to move away, but he made a grab and held her closer. She panicked and struggled to free herself by kicking him hard between the legs. Billy yelled and fell back clutching himself. He caught her coat lapel in his hand and in falling it ripped down to the button beneath, making her lose her balance and fall into the damp undergrowth.

11

"You little bugger. Don't think you'll get away with this, Ada-bloody-Skipton, or whatever your name is. I'll get even with you. No lass leads me on and then leaves without coming up with the goods."

He was flaming mad, a man scorned, but for a time her blow had crippled him and she was able to get to her feet and brush herself down. Her skirt was creased and marked with the damp brown earth. But she ran — ran as fast as her feet would carry her, until she reached the safety of the main street.

What a sight she looked — dishevelled, torn and dirty. Desperately she tried to tidy herself up, but through the reflection of a shop window she saw Lily and a group of girls coming towards her.

CHAPTER TWO

Ada, Lily and the rest of the lasses stared at one another in utter disbelief. There was no way the mess she was in could be hidden: her torn jacket, her hat askew, hair loose and almost falling down, and, the most tell-tale of all, the mucky dark patch of mud on her skirt.

"What the bloody hell have you been up to, Ada? My God, you don't half look a sight."

Ada coloured up, but tried to brush it aside with, "Oh, it was nowt. I slipped and fell into them bushes." The words came out, but there was no way she could hide her embarrassment.

The lasses sniggered. "Now I've heard it all. I bet you fell into them bushes. More like Billy Acton pushed you. We might believe you, but thousands wouldn't." They grinned, pointing and mocking.

Lily joined them at first and then, seeing how upset Ada was, she quickly rushed to her defence and made to help get her tidy and clean.

"It's all right Lily, I can manage." She spoke brusquely, almost in tears, but she managed to square her shoulders and, holding her head high, marched down the street.

My God, what on earth had she been thinking off, and who would believe her that nothing had happened between her and Billy. He had a right reputation and it was always the bloke that folk took notice of. What would Mam say? And, more important, what a way to disgrace Wilf's memory — and on her first day's outing and all.

It wasn't as if she even liked Billy. In fact she loathed him — he was awful. And she knew full well it would be all round the laundry the next day. How was she going to cope with all the gossip and the shame?

Lily had left the others and was walking at her side. Suddenly Ada stopped, grabbed her arm and looking her straight in the face said, "Nowt happened Lily. Honest — nowt. I just went a bit daft for a minute. But I only let him kiss me. You do believe me don't you?"

Her voice was desperate and Lily could see tears welling up in her eyes. "I do, love. Yes I believe you. I know for one thing it's your poorly week. Remember we are both on at the same time? You couldn't get up to owt in that state."

Relief swept through Ada. Oh thank God. She'd forgotten about having her monthlies. And now Mam would know for certain that nowt had happened. As for the others — well — that was a bit different. She couldn't very well give them intimate details of her bodily functions. You didn't talk about such things out in the open.

"Did he try owt on though? He's a right randy bugger is Billy." Lily was looking for a reason to explain Ada's crumpled mess.

"It wasn't like that, Lily. It wasn't like that at all. I don't know what the devil came over me. I let him kiss me like Wilf used to, but only for a few minutes. And then when he tried to go further I brought my knee up. I didn't want owt like that — least of all with him. But it was funny, Lily. I wanted to be kissed and held again, to know what it feels like to have a man's arms around me. Well, that's what started it all. It was as much my fault as his, if truth's known." Being so utterly honest, Ada was not going to put all the blame on Billy.

"All right, love. Forget it now. Come on, let's get you tidied up and then go and get our dinners off the bus."

With the help of hankies, water from the horse drinking trough and a couple of safety pins they managed to made Ada look presentable. But she knew what it would be like on the journey home — and she was right. The lasses had spread the word and they sniggered and nudged one another, talking in whispers about her and Billy.

He sat smirking and making the most of it. It was quite a feather in his cap if they thought he had got anywhere with Ada Tanner. If that's what they thought then let them get on with it. Better than telling them what had really gone on and how she had spurned him.

Ada had had more than enough of the mocking and snide remarks by the time the bus got back to Brid and she refused to go for the fish and chip supper.

"Well, you're coming Ada, whether you like it or not. Don't let them get to you, Ada. They'll only think the worst if you don't come." Lily had a point there and so, reluctantly, she went, pushing each mouthful down as if it would choke her.

She couldn't believe it when Billy Acton came to her outside the fish and chip shop, putting his arms around her — in front of them all — and saying loudly, "I shan't forget our walk in the woods in a hurry, Ada. We saw a sight more than the rhododendrons, didn't we?"

She could have killed him, but instead, with all the dignity she could muster, pushed him away without saying a word.

She felt rather than saw her mother's startled look as she walked into the house. Thank God it was nearly dark and they hadn't lit the gas mantles yet.

She glared at Esther, who bit her lip to stop herself from saying what was on her mind. Instead, she simply asked if Ada had enjoyed herself and then busied herself getting a cup of tea.

Ada made quickly for the stairs and rushed up to her room where she flung off her clothes as if they were infected.

"Damn you, Ada Tanner. Damn you, you silly bitch. What the hell were you thinking on?" She sat down on the bed and sobbed out the words. She was so ashamed — ashamed for herself, for her Mam and, most of all, for Wilf.

She heard murmurings downstairs and then the sound of her Mam's laboured breath as she climbed the stairs.

Esther stood at the bedroom door and looked down at her daughter sobbing so helplessly on the bed. "What's up lass? Come on, don't take on so. Tell Mam what's bothering you so."

Esther sat down on the bed and Ada, through her sobs, tried to tell the whole sad story. She spared herself nothing not even a large share of the blame.

"What am I going to do Mam? I shan't ever forgive myself. And what will laundry bosses and our lasses say?"

"They won't say owt — none of 'em — not if I'm around. I know you are not a bad lass — not like that. But temptation comes to us all at some time. I'm only too glad you didn't go any further. Come on, let's have a cup of tea, eh?"

Together they went downstairs to join the rest of the family who, though they were bursting with curiosity, dare not say a word when they saw the look on Esther's face. They would be told when she was ready to do so and not before — and certainly not in front ofSAda.

The next day Ada knew she was the talk of the laundry. And by hek, they were making a meal of it. Ada Tanner — that stuck up bitch who thought she was something better, and Billy Acton — well, that put everything in the shade.

She was waiting to be called into the office and it was no surprise when, during the morning break, Mrs. Price came and asked her to take tea with her and her husband.

"Well, Ada, what's all this I've been hearing? Not very nice gossip going around the laundry this morning about you and Billy Acton. I wouldn't have thought he was your cup of tea. But more to the

15

point, I can't have my senior staff being talked about in his way. You lose the respect and then the control of the girls. That does not do at all."

Mrs. Price gazed at her loftily as she raised the china cup to her lips. In truth, Ada felt it wasn't really any of her ruddy business. What she did in her own time was nowt to do with work, or anybody else for that matter. She was a free agent. Still, they had been good to her and given her promotion and so, briefly, she told her the outline of what had happened, trying to make light of the whole thing.

Mr. Price smiled up at her and said he had never thought Ada was a girl like that.

"And I'm not either, so you can stop eyeing me up and down," Ada snapped and walked out of the office. She knew Price and if he thought there was owt going he'd be in as quick as a shot.

Mrs. Price decided not to belabour the point. Ada was a good worker and she didn't want to lose her. Better to let the matter drop. But of course, things are not always as easy and straightforward as that.

In the early afternoon when Ada was going round inspecting, she stopped by Molly Drayton, who was working one of the huge roller mangles that pressed the sheets. She watched as the girl deliberately creased a sheet, knowing very well that she was challenging Ada to correct the mistake.

"Straighten that out, Molly." Ada spoke calmly sensing a storm brewing.

"Who the hell do you reckon you are to tell me what to do? You want to look after your own business. You're no better than us, Ada Tanner. You're just the same underneath all that Hikey top." She rounded on Ada and glared into her face.

"Shut your trap Molly and get on with it. It's nowt to do with you. If you looked after your bloke he wouldn't need to roam. Maybe you are a bit too free with your favours and he's not that keen on cheap goods. Happen that's why he's not wed you afore now." The words were out before Ada could stop them and she tried to add, "Anyway, I thought you two had finished."

"We're finished all right, and you know why, because he's got me wrong. I'm in trouble and he won't wed me and what you did on that trip didn't help, you bitch. He's allust had an eye for you and now you've took him from me." Molly started to scream and made to attack Ada by pulling her hair.

16

Ada put up both hands to defend herself and pushed Molly, who fell into the still working machine.

It was a nightmare. Molly's arm got caught up with the sheet and was churned into the twisting rollers. Her screams rang through the laundry, rising above the noise of the machines. The torment tore into Ada's heart and she forgot all the bitterness of a few moments ago and swiftly moved forward to stop the machine.

When she opened the rollers, Molly's arm was a mass of bloody mangled pulp, still caught in the machine. Ada stood mesmerised and then realised that a crowd had gathered and stood looking at her in silent accusation.

They moved foward and for a minute she thought they were going to attack her. Panic rose in her throat and her heart beat so loud she thought they would hear her above the murmurings of anger.

"Bloody hell, what's happened now? Come on, let's get the lass down to Lloyd's hospital." Good old Lily had come to her side and distracted the crowd.

"Yes. Yes — come on Lil — give us a hand."

Ada pulled herself together and moved towards Molly.

"Leave her alone, Ada. I think you've done enough. I'll take over now. Get back to work the rest of you." Mrs. Price marched forward and spoke angrily.

"It wasn't her fault. Molly went for her. I saw it," Lily defended.

"Well, it was certainly Ada who started the whole thing off by getting mixed up with Billy Acton yesterday. I'll see you later in the office. Just get on with what you were doing."

Lily and Mrs. Price attended to Molly, who had by now been brought round.

Ada had had enough, and taking no notice of anyone, she went into the cloakroom, took off her apron and cap and went home. She wanted to see her Mam and she ran down the street as fast as her heels could carry her. Mam would make it all right again. She stumbled through the door in a state of confusion and tears and blurted out her troubles to her Mam.

"Well, they can't blame you for what happened, bairn, and they won't either or they'll have me to deal with. It couldn't be your fault, and anyway they all know you wouldn't do that to anybody." She rose to her daughter's defence and tried to give her some comfort.

When Thom heard the story he threatened to go to the laundry and sort it all out. "I'll settle Billy Acton and that Price woman and all. Fancy saying that after the way you've worked your guts out for them. By hell, I'll settle her."

Esther restrained him telling him quietly that Ada was a married woman. It was her business and they must deal with it as she would wish.

The next morning she did not know whether to go to work or not. How could she face them all?

"Come on, our Ada, I'll take you, just like I did when you got into trouble at school. If they say owt, I'll thump 'em." Her sister Aggie took her arm and tried to make her laugh.

"What was it like yesterday afternoon. Is Molly badly hurt?" Ada asked.

"I don't honestly know. I kept out of the way and nipped home quick down the back alley. Come on, she'll never sack you."

Aggie had read her thoughts and Ada knew she was right. Mrs. Price would never sack her if she could help it for there was no-one else who could take over like Ada could. But all the same, things were going to be rough.

In the end it was the girls who forced the decision on her. They sent her to Coventry and just ignored everything she asked them to do. Molly was not as badly hurt as they had at first thought, but there was no doubt that her arm would be disabled for months, if not forever. It would be a long time before she could work again.

"Don't take on. It'll all blow over. Stick it out, Ada," Lily begged.

But it was no use. When the dinner time siren sounded, Ada went into the office and asked for her cards. At first Mrs. Price protested, but she could see that Ada had made up her mind to leave.

"I can't pay you any wages for this week, not with you going without giving notice," she said, snottily.

"That's all right, Missus. Give them to Molly. She'll need them, 'cos I know damn well you won't pay her owt."

As she came out of the office she saw Aggie waiting by the big doors. "Have you finished then?" she asked, and Ada told her what had happened.

"Hang on a minute then, I'm coming with you." And without any more ado she walked into the office and asked the astonished Mrs. Price for her cards too.

"But why, Aggie? What has happened is nothing to do with you. You don't have to leave."

"No, and neither did our Ada if you'd stood by her. By hell, I'll

18

tell you one thing missus, you'll miss her a damn sight more than she'll miss you. I'm going with our Ada. Maybe we've both been here a bit too long."

She went outside, and tucking her arm into Ada's, they walked as straight as dies down the street until they were out of sight of the staring eyes of the girls who had come outside to see what was going on.

"Well, now I've got us into a right mess. What are we going to do now, our Aggie? We've got to find work or how are we going to manage?"

"I'll tell you what we are going to do, Ada Tanner, we are going to set up on our own as we've often said we would. If we can work our fingers to the bone for old Price, we can do it for ourselves — and earn a damn sight more and all."

Ada's heart went out to her sister and the thought of setting up in business together. She was so ashamed and heartbroken at what had happened as a result of a few moments of thoughtlessness. It was all over town now. Polly and Gertie would hardly speak to her and many who had known her all their lives ignored her as she went about town. She felt all the whispers and glances cutting into her soul.

But none of the family blamed her. They daren't or they'd have Esther and Thom to deal with. She knew they were upset, but they would stand by her. Aggie had just shown how much by her actions alone. Her throat ached as she thought of their loving support.

But what now? Dear God, when would it all end? First Wilf, then this do with Billy Acton, then Molly, and now she was virtually out of work. Maybe Aggie was right. Maybe it was time to make a fresh start. After all nowt lasts forever — not life and not even bad fortune.

Maybe things would be better now. God knew, she'd had enough sadness to last a lifetime.

CHAPTER THREE

If anyone had ever tried to tell her, Ada would never have believed them that setting up a business would be such an enormous undertaking. It seemed to take up every minute of her day. Either she or Aggie would be arranging or organising: the money, machines, and, of course, the customers.

The good thing was that it did help to take the Billy Acton business off her mind a little bit. But no matter what she was doing, always at the back of her mind it lingered, making her feel guilty and unclean. So much so, that she would shrug her shoulders as if trying to shake off the guilt and dirt. She even got nervous about going out and although Esther told her it would be a nine day's wonder, she stayed in unless it was absolutely necessary for her to cross the door.

More than anything the worry about Molly and her injury played on her mind. "I feel I ought to do something for the lass, take her some money or summat. Laundry won't give her owt and after all, Mam, it was a bit my fault," she said.

"I'm sorry, Ada. I don't think so. If you do take her owt it'll make out that you are to blame. And whatever you feel right now, let me tell you my lass, you're not. That bloke was to blame for it all, not you. It's all nearly died down now so take my advice and let it rest."

But being Ada she couldn't let it rest and she took herself off one morning to the Yorkshire Penny Bank and withdrew fifty pounds.

"More for the business, Mrs. Tanner?" The cashier tried to be friendly. She scowled at up at him and told him to mind his business and just get on with his job.

She couldn't have explained to anybody why, but she felt so nervous, as if she was committing a crime. As she walked up to Molly's home she had to pass Polly's and she became so agitated that she was almost running as she passed the door.

Should she call in? No, best not. Polly hadn't been too kind about the whole incident, feeling it was an insult to Wilf's memory. As for Gertie, well, she had been a true friend in her faith of Ada's innocence but, at the moment, she was too busy getting ready to go into training as a nurse. Since Alf had been killed she had been set on this one purpose — to be a nurse. And where was she going? To Lloyd's so she could be near her Mam? Not on your life. She was off to Barnsley to be near Alf's folks. Ada couldn't make that out. It wasn't as if she knew them at all. And who was going to see to Polly?

Well, she knew the answer to that all right — that is if Polly ever gave her a chance to explain what had happened and maybe come round a bit. Oh, it would have been so comforting to be able to call in for a few words and a cup of tea. She really missed the old girl.

At last she was at Molly's house and she stood for a moment before banging on the front door, which was wedged open by a piece of brick.

Nobody answered, and popping her head round the door, she called out, "Anybody in then?"

Ginny Drayton was coming down the narrow stairs that led into the kitchen when she saw Ada, half in and half out of the door. Her mouth dropped open in undisguised amazement.

"What do you want here Ada Skipton?" Her manner was aggressive and blunt.

"My name's — oh bugger it, never mind. I've come to have a word with your Molly. Is she in?"

Molly had quietly followed Ginny down the steps and startled Ada by confronting her. Her arm was still in a sling resting upon her swollen belly. God, she'd forgotten the lass was expecting as well. It looked as if the bairn was nearly due and all.

For a moment, the thought of asking if she could take the bairn passed through her mind. No, that would be daft. But at times she got so bewildered without Wilf at her side that things got mixed up. She thought of Alf's sister at Barnsley — and the bairn she thought might be Wilf's. That had nowt to do with this lot. What the hell was she thinking about?

"I'd have thought you'd have more about you than to come up here and mix with us, Mrs. Tanner." Molly emphasised the words.

Ada sighed, almost spent with the effort of it all. "I haven't come here to row, Molly. I've come to try and help — daft as it may seem. I know you won't be getting much, if owt, from laundry and I just thought . . . " The words trailed into silence and the three women stood looking at each other.

"How do you mean, help?" Molly spoke more gently now. She could see it had taken a lot for Ada to come and see her and although she was a bit rough and blunt, Molly would never bear a grudge.

"Well, I expect you know as most people seem to think they do that I'm not without a bob or two and — and I'd like to give you a bit towards your keep and getting ready for the bairn like."

21

"Don't you bother about the bairn. I'll see to it as how him that's responsible will pay for that little lark."

"I've no doubt about that lass, but there's still your keep and you look as though you could do with a bit of help."

Molly half smiled at her. "Nay lass — it's all right — you're not the 'onny one to have a bit about them you know. I've not got money, but I've got pride. You keep your help. We'll manage, won't we, Mam?"

Ginny was not so sure. Keeping a strapping lass like Molly took some managing and though she would never sponge she was not going to look a gift horse in the mouth.

"Well, let's talk it over with a cup of tea shall we? Come inside proper Ada and sit yourself down." She gave her daughter a sideways glance, trying to get her to think before she turned down the offer.

Ada could see how things were going and though she wasn't going to be taken for a mug, she wanted the whole thing off her mind. "No thanks. I'm not going to waste your time Mrs. Drayton, I know how you like to get on. I've brought fifty quid — tek it or leave it." Her voice was firm as she opened her purse and proferred the money.

Ginny made to take it out of her hand, but Molly stepped forward and brushed her aside.

"Leave it Mam. Ada wasn't to blame for owt. It were my bloody temper that caused this." She tapped her arm. "I'll not tek owt I'm not entitled to."

"Molly, I want you to have it. What happened was both our faults — well, more mine really, for what happened with Billy. Take it lass. I would feel a sight better if you did."

"As you say — if it were anybody's fault it were Billy's and I'm not going to say as I couldn't do with the money. But I'll not take fifty quid, not from a working lass, and that's what you are Ada, whether you like to think so or not. You're just like the rest of us." The words would have been harsh and unkind had not her voice and smile been soft.

"Please Molly," Ada pleaded and she looked at Ginny for help.

Molly looked at them both. "I'll tell you what. Give us twenty-five quid and we'll call matter settled here and now. That way both of you will be satisfied."

Ada smiled in relief and counted out the money. "I don't want

22

anybody else to hear of this Molly, and Ginny. Keep your mouth shut. Nobody's to know — not Billy — or any of our lot either — understand?"

"If that's the way, then it's fine by me lass. And Ada, thanks. You're all right. I never did really hold you to blame you know."

Molly took the money and without another word Ada left with Ginny's words ringing in her ears, as she shouted at her daughter for not taking the lot. "You daft bitch. That lot would have set us up just right."

But it was over. Ada's conscience was eased and she could now face up to getting on with her life.

At home Aggie and Esther noticed how she had brightened up and although nobody said owt Esther had an idea that somehow, in her funny way, Ada had put things right. Anyway, it was Ada's business. She was old enough to know what she was about and certainly no fool: the way she was going about setting up in business had shown that.

Premises had been a bit of a problem. That is, premises with the right facilities like water, gas and drying areas included.

"Why don't you tek our big washhouse over? You can have it rent free if you'll do our washing." Thom half laughed as he suggested it.

Ada thought it was a splendid idea and agreed to do all the family's wash.

"Eh, that will be a help. I get tired on wash days now, especially if it's wet," Esther said, and Ada looked at her Mam, realising for the first time that she was beginning to show her age. Come to think of it, she was nigh on seventy, but she'd never thought of her Mam as old, not in that way.

The remark about wet wash days brought home the problem of drying during the winter months, but again Thom came to the rescue and said they could enclose the part under the big glass roof that he had used as a greenhouse. It was huge, covering most of one side of the yard.

"But what about your blessed plants, Dad?" Aggie asked.

"Well, I'm getting a bit past all that now. The aspidistra can come inside, but as for the rest, well I don't really want the bother of looking after them all now."

This time Ada looked at her Dad in surprise. It was the first time either of them had said owt about being tired and getting on a bit. Maybe this was Dad's way of helping the lasses. Ada put her arms round him and snuggled into his now snow-white beard. She giggled like a child as the softness tickled her face.

"By hek, that's a sound to gladden my heart. I've not heard you laugh, Ada, for many a long day," he said, and for the first time in many a month Esther's heart warmed too. Maybe all this sadness was going to pass over after all. But it had taken its toll on her more than she liked to admit.

Ada took on the roll of administrator and financier and put up the money for most of the equipment they needed.

"We'll have it done proper and all. I'll go down to Ralph Tinker and get him to set it all up legal and proper like."

"Why, Ada, we're sisters, we don't need to be so business like. I'd manage with dolly tubs and pegs or poshers to start with."

"No. If we are going to do it, it will be done proper. I've ordered two hand washing machines."

"Well, if you say so Ada, and there's no doubt they'll save a lot of time and work."

Ralph Tinker was surprised when he saw Ada's name on his appointment list. Realising that he would get nowhere in his pursuit of Ada he had buried himself in his work and tried — and almost succeeded — in putting her out of his mind. But now, as he thought of her, his heart warmed with excitement at the thought of seeing her again.

As she stepped into his office he saw immediately that she was even thinner than ever. He was sure, given the chance, he could span her waist with his hands. He held them tightly behind his back to prevent himself from doing just that for Ada, as ever, turned his heart over as her tiny face set in its usual firm manner gazed up at him.

"I'm setting up in laundry business. I expect you've heard all gossip, but that's over and done with. I want you to set up the legal part for me and our Aggie."

The words tumbled out and he had to suppress a smile. She was still a firework was Ada.

"Well at least sit down and tell me all about it. Would you like a cup of tea?"

He was surprised when she accepted and almost thankfully sat down in the proffered chair.

"Well now, tell me all about it, Ada. What brought this about?"

She stared at him and opening her mouth tried to speak. The words would not come. She tried again and her voice got stuck inside her throat. All that emerged was a strangled sob.

Ralph got up and stood beside her, placing his hand on her shoulder. "Ada," he said softly. "What is it?"

To his amazement she broke down in wild sobs. "Oh why, why did he have to die? I wouldn't have got into such a mess if Wilf had been here. Bugger the Kaiser," and sobbing, she blurted out the whole story.

"There was nowt in it, Sir, not with Billy Acton. I don't — I've never loved anybody but Wilf. It was just that I was so lonely, so empty like."

Ralph allowed himself to stroke her hair, tentatively at first, in case he frightened her.

"I know that, Ada. And please, after all this time, can't you call me Ralph? You must know how I feel about you, how I've always felt about you. This may not be the moment, but I know there's never been anyone for you but Wilf — I know that to my sorrow."

Startled, she looked up at him. "You mean, you fancied me, really like?"

"Really like," he mimicked.

"Well, I'll be buggered." She sat for a minute in silence. "It's very nice of you Sir — Ralph — but you've not a cat in hell's chance you know. I'll love Wilf till the day I die. But you can help me — with the business like." She smiled through her tears.

After several cups of tea and a few more tears mingled with a little laughter they got the official papers organised. She was glad now that she had come to Ralph, glad that he had not for one moment doubted her in all this sorry mess and a little surprised at his admission. But then, she was learning that fellers were a bit funny, especially when they thought a woman was on her own and a bit lonely.

"Right, now that's done I'll get the papers drawn up and you and your sister can come down and sign them. Is that all right with you, Ada?"

"Oh yes, Sir, that's fine, Sir — and Sir — er Ralph — thank you, thank you for everything."

"There is nothing to thank me for Ada. Just remember I am here if ever needed."

She smiled as he opened the door for her and looking at him

cheekily said: "Just as long as you don't get any fancy ideas, that's all Sir. I don't want any more bother."

As she walked home she felt warmed by what had happened. Oh she didn't want any doings with Ralph Tinker, not in that way. But she knew he would be a friend if ever she needed one, and that felt good.

She had come to the conclusion that, sometimes, a woman needed a man around to support her.

CHAPTER FOUR

When she totted up just how much she'd put into the business she began to have a few qualms. The laundry room, as they called it, looked like a miniature laundry, and with the most up-to-date equipment.

But her worries were unfounded. Following Ralph's advice, she had sent out printed notices to all possible customers, taking care not to poach on any of the Bridlington Steam Laundry ones. That wouldn't have been right. But in her usual way, she saw to it that they all knew. She placed an advertisement in the *Free Press* and *Chronicle*, with the starting date in double letters.

It took only a few weeks for the work to come pouring in. No matter what gossip had gone before, Ada and Aggie had a good reputation for their work. Soon all the churches were sending their surplices in and the big houses all their fine work. It got to the stage when Mrs. Price came down with a proposition for them to take on her hand work because with her two best girls gone, so had the standard of work.

"We'll take it in, and pay you a proportional rate," said Mrs. Price.

"We'll take it on my rates or not at all. Folk that send that kind of work down can afford to pay for it," Ada snapped. And she got her way. She had the upper hand.

At first the dealings were all in cash and then one or two of the housekeepers asked for monthly statements to be sent — it would be more convenient that way. Ada had taken on being the brains of the business and decided to do this, but, canny in her way, made an extra charge for the paper work involved.

"We ought to have a proper name, you know, not just *St. John Street Laundry*. That doesn't sound like a proper business," she said.

"Well, I could think of one, but we couldn't use it," Aggie laughed.

The girls were getting along fine. They never argued about who did what, and surprised even themselves at the amount of work they got through. On Tuesdays and Thursdays Cissie came in to help with the scrubbing down, sorting and a bit of ironing. She had five young 'uns and the money came in very handy.

They had a conference with Esther and Thom one teatime about the name and finally came up with "*Snow White Laundry*."

"That says it just right. All your work is snow white," Esther smiled.

"Not the colours I hope, Mam," Aggie laughed.

But they took the name and so on the top of all the correspondence and bills they had that printed — at first by Thom using his beloved John Bull outfit. Underneath, in small letters, he put "Proprietors:- Ada Tanner. Agnes Skipton."

"That looks right grand, Dad. Makes us look proper posh," Ada laughed.

But it made things look more official and business like, which pleased her. She looked set to become a real business woman. But at times Esther would see a look in her eye as she saw couples walking down the street together. Her heart still ached for Wilf and would for some time to come.

"Doing this Mam, makes me feel better you know, as if I'm fulfilling a promise to Wilf. We built so much hope on a business together, I feel I'm keeping that promise."

Esther knew what she meant, and her heart ached. Life for her and Thom had not been quite the same since the war and folk weren't the same any more. The world was changing too fast for them.

Ada never bothered with men at all, in fact she very rarely went out, except perhaps at weekends to walk along the sea front with Aggie and look at the new sea wall that was being built.

"I wonder what she's doing with all that money? She must be worth a bob or two now," Thom remarked to Esther.

"Well, I know she's good to our Cissie. The bairns don't want for anything and she's pretty good to old Polly now that Gertie's down in London. Oh, I'm glad they made up after that Billy Acton business. Polly hasn't anybody close, and our Ada is a real comfort to her."

Gertie had, like Ada, done exceptionally well, better than she'd have done if she'd married Alf Aylward, Ada often said. She found out that it was not a good idea to have gone to Barnsley as things did not turn out as she would have wished and she had asked for, and been given, a transfer to a big London teaching hospital and was doing very well. Ada thought fate very odd. Would she or Gertie have been successful had their men come home? She doubted it, but she'd have given it all up for Wilf.

"But would you, Ada, would you really, if he'd come back?" Ada knew Gertie was right. If Wilf had come back, she'd have been her old pushing self.

"I wouldn't have done anything because I didn't know anything then. One thing Alf's death did for me was to open my eyes to a world outside. If it hadn't been for the war I'd still be up at them washtubs," Gertie said.

Ada visited Polly at least once a week. She did her shopping and paid a neighbour to keep the house tidy. It was, in a way, making up for the loss of her lads and, maybe, the bitterness of the Billy Acton and Molly episode.

Polly would often say she didn't know what she'd do without her. Sometimes she got maudlin and begged forgiveness for misjudging her. Ada just patted her hand and told her not to bother herself, it was over and done with now.

She was that busy with work and seeing to Polly that she never noticed how Esther had been failing. Every morning she would make the lasses a cup of Camp coffee round about eleven and then go to the door and call them in. Aggie had noticed that these days she tired easily, but never thought to mention it. Surely they too must have seen the drawn face and dark-rimmed eyes.

But one morning the usual call did not come. Ada looked up from the starching bowl and remarked to Aggie that her throat was parched.

"See if Mam's ready yet?" Aggie went into the kitchen to find Esther still sitting in her armchair.

"Are you all right, Mam? We wondered if the drink was ready yet," she asked.

"Oh yes, yes I'm fine. Just a mite tired, love. I'll get drink now. You go and fetch Ada in."

"I don't think Mam's well. I think we ought to get her down to the doctor," Aggie told Ada.

"Maybe she needs a tonic. We'll have a word with Dad," Ada promised and they went in for coffee.

Aggie looked down at hers and thought the milk had gone sour. Ada took a mouthful and spat it out, all over the clean white tablecloth.

"Hell's bells! What's up with this coffee, Mam? Either milk's gone sour or coffee's off," and she went to get a drink of water to wash away the bitter taste.

Aggie tried hers and then ran to spit it out.

29

"Where's the bottle, Mam? It wants chucking out."

She took the bottle from Esther and went outside to the dustbin. She was just about to put the lid on when she looked at the offending bottle and saw that it did not have the familiar Scots figure on the label. This was the only way Esther could recognise most things, not being able to read. Aggie looked at the label and saw it was gravy browning and not coffee.

"Ada, Ada come here a minute," she called and showed her the bottle.

"I've never known Mam get owt wrong like this afore in my life, have you? You're right, Aggie, summat's up with her. I'll get Dad to have a word and we'll tek her down to surgery."

They spoke to Thom and he agreed with them. "I've been bothered for a bit, but I didn't want to frighten Esther or worry you two, you've enough on as it is," he said.

Getting her to do as they asked might be quite another thing though. "The lasses don't think you're looking too well, lass, and they think as how we ought to see doctor and get you a tonic or summat," he said, trying not to make too much of things.

"Well, I have been feeling a bit funny lately. I've been that tired and often get a bad head — and me legs go funny," Esther answered and surprisingly made no trouble about seeing the doctor.

The doctor's opinion was that it could be a clot of blood and that Esther was to have a few days in bed on complete rest to let it hopefully disperse.

All the family made a fuss of her and took it in turns to see to things. They'd never known Mam not to be up and busy about the place, and it didn't feel right her being upstairs in bed. Esther only stayed in bed for confinements and they teased her about this.

"Well, if I am, none of you will need to work again. They'd put me in a circus and travel me," she laughed.

Thom was like a lost sheep, and kept wandering about the place and poking around.

"He needs to be occupied," Ada said to Aggie and set him on making new posts for indoor drying. They didn't really need them but it kept his mind busy for a while.

Esther was not making the progress that Ada thought she should and she got uneasy. She mentioned it to Aggie and they decided to take it upon themselves to go down to the doctor's and see if there was anything more that could be done. He seemed to expect the visit and suggested a specialist from Hull should be called in as soon as possible.

"I'm afraid that will cost ten guineas," he told them.

"Don't you bother about money, doctor, that won't hurt us, and anyway I'll pay for it myself. I owe Mam more than money," Ada replied.

But the family wouldn't have that and each of them chipped in with a share for the specialist.

He arrived one Wednesday afternoon. Aggie and Ada rushed through the work so they could talk to him and find out what ailed their Mam. He went upstairs, and examined Esther thoroughly while they stood waiting for him on the landing.

"Let's go downstairs. I don't like talking about a patient if there is any chance that they can hear me," he whispered.

"What's up then, doctor? It's not serious is it?" Ada took on the role of spokesman.

"I'm afraid it is. There appears to be an embolism, a clot of blood, that has damaged the heart. I am most awfully sorry, but I have to tell you that there is nothing I can do for your Mother."

The words stunned them. Not Mam — Mam was always — they couldn't do without Mam.

"Money's no object. We can afford to pay for anything you can do," Ada spoke earnestly, grabbing his arm to emphasise her words.

"My dear, I wish there was something I could do, but there is nothing — nothing. It is only a matter of time."

Numbed, they saw him to the door and then went into the kitchen where Thom sat in his chair. Ada looked across at Mam's empty chair and the void churned at her insides. The room became filled with gloom as they tried, gently, to tell him that his beloved Esther was very ill.

He didn't say much, but as he took his old pipe out of his pocket and tried to light it Ada saw his hands were shaking and tears began to roll down his weathered old cheeks.

Aggie started to sob and Ada went to Thom and stroked his head.

"She's been all the world to me has Esther. God broke the mould when he made her. I hope God will take her quick and not let her suffer. I don't want that, Ada, and I hope he takes me at the same time and all. I don't want to be without my little Esther."

"It'll be all right, Dad. We'll get her mended, you'll see. Mam's not one for giving in." Ada tried to comfort him, and herself, but

31

deep in her heart she knew that Mam would not be with them much longer.

A void engulfed her again, as it had when she had received the telegram about Wilf — a dark echoing void that forebode doom and ached within her.

CHAPTER FIVE

After the visit of the specialist, Esther seemed to Ada to almost give up, as if she was tired of life.

She mentioned her feelings to Aggie, as they bent over the churning washing machine. "But she should be enjoying life now, shouldn't she, not giving up? She and Dad could have a holiday together, or one of us could take them. It's not as if any of us are in need. Our Isabella's got her hands full, I know, with George being a bit funny after his war do. But crikey, they'd be the first to tip the brass. What do you reckon?"

Aggie waited a long time before answering, giving, at least appearing to give, all her attention to the surplices from Trinity Church.

Ada got impatient and spoke harshly. "Aggie?"

Aggie stretched and stood up, folded her arms and looked straight at her sister. "Well, you might not like this, our Ada, but, well, you've always been so taken with what you're doing, you never gave a lot of thought to owt or anybody else. Now don't get ikey with me. If you think, you'll be honest and know it's the truth. First there was that place you and Wilf were planning on — and then when he got killed you thought of nowt else but your grief. There were millions of others, Ada. But no, Ada Tanner were worst done by."

As Ada remained silent Aggie continued: "And then Bily Acton. Well, least said about that the better. But you played right into his hands you know. And then Molly. Oh, I know it wasn't your fault lass. I shouldn't be here working beside you if it was. But you did shove your way through it all, and to hell with owt or anybody else. If I hadn't come in with you, you'd have given Mam no end to do — and expected her to do it and all. Do you know what we call you, Ada?" She broke off to laugh kindly.

"No, and I don't bloody well care. If you want owt you've got to go out and get it. Dad always said that, and I'm not doing too badly. You've got to admit."

"We're proud of you, Ada, all of us. You've always been a little fighter, but be honest now, you were born with a bowler hat on your head weren't you?"

"Now that's a bit of Dad. He always says that foremen are born with bowler hats tight on their heads. Does he say that as well?"

33

As she answered, Ada's face had to surrender to the mirth within her. A foreman, eh, that's what they called her? Well, better that than owt else.

"Yes, even Dad. When you get in one of your idea moods we all say 'here comes the bowler hat.' You do try to manage folk to your way you know. It can be a bit trying and tiring at times."

Ada thought for a moment and then asked sharply, "You're not saying that it's me that's caused Mam to be poorly are you?"

Aggie dried her hands and with arms still steaming from the hot water went over to Ada and placed her arms around her shoulders. "No, we are not, but what with Stanley having open house to the other lads' wives when they wanted to come and stop, feeding us lot while we slaved, then she felt for Gertie and young Alfie, for Polly and for Wilf and all that bother — she's getting on you know. You seem to forget that. She's had seventeen bairns and brought up sixteen — and a load of grandbairns and all. You can't expect so much, Ada. Let her rest in her own way. Rest might be just what she needs — a good long rest."

Ada had to agree, but Aggie had made her feel more than guilty. Wilf had often said that she was bossy, that she went roughshod if she wanted owt. Had she been like that with him? Did Mam think that's how she was? Please God, no. She worshipped her Mam, and wouldn't hurt a hair on her head.

Thom had given up work now. He could have stayed on after the war, but he too was ready for a rest and now that Esther was poorly he wanted to be near her all the time.

Cissie came and did the housework; Isabella sent down enough food to feed an army; and Ada and Aggie — well they were a great comfort. They were a right pair of devils and if it hadn't been for their mischievous humour he felt sometimes he would have gone mad.

The ache of seeing Esther just laid there day after day felt like a brick in his stomach. But she seemed at peace and not in pain and that was all he could hope for. In the afternoons he would go and sit with her, pulling back the lace curtains so that they could look through the window on to the busy street where they had spent so much of their lives, indeed all their married life. The road had been widened and they would talk endlessly about the houses that used to be there, and the people who had been neighbours and friends.

Johnny Sawden and Maria, both gone now. Johnny had died

34

very suddenly, but he had left all his house and money to Maria. "But she didn't last long after him, did she, Thom? Four months and we were stood at her graveside. Eh, it's a funny old lot, isn't it, lad?"

Maria had wanted to will everything to Thom and Esther. "You've been that good, and I know Johnny would want it too."

But Thom would have none of it. What did they need at their age? The family would provide what bit he and Esther couldn't manage.

They had deliberated long and deeply upon the best place to leave the money and finally, mainly in remembrance of his lad and his wife, had decided to leave it to the orphans home. Johnny had been one, hadn't he? Yes, that would be fitting. When it was all finalised they were astonished at the amount — almost fifty thousand pounds.

"By hek, lass, we shan't have owt like that to leave, shall we?" Thom had laughed.

"No, but we'll have a lot of love and enough folk to keep Brid going for a year or two," Esther replied.

That warmed Thom, the thought of leaving generations to follow the footprints he had laid.

During the following days Ada made a special effort to see her Mam. She went up to Lake's and bought her little dainty cakes, arrowroot biscuits, which were one of Esther's favourites, and violet and mint cachous to sweeten her mouth.

"You spoil me, our Ada," Esther would say, and Ada's throat would contract as she recalled Aggie's words.

After three weeks had passed, Ada's hopes began to rise. Maybe the specialist had been wrong. They did make mistakes sometimes, didn't they? Maybe Mam would recover after all.

Her hopes were dashed one Friday afternoon when Cissie and Aggie were bathing Esther and changing the bed. It was tiring, but this time more so. When they had finished Esther flopped back on the pillows and sighed deeply.

"Fetch Dad and our Ada up will you?" she asked, her voice barely a whisper. Aggie frowned and did as her Mam asked.

The moment she stepped into the bedroom Ada knew that this was the end.

"What is it, hunny?" Thom asked and went to sit on the bed.

"I want to tell you all summat. Sit me up Thom, so that I can see you all," Esther answered.

35

He did as she asked and then she leaned forward and grasped his hand tightly. "It's time I was going to Jesus. No, no, I don't want any of you to say owt. I know it's time and there's nowt to be done. What I want to do is have my wishes carried out. I want Jackie Mainprize to be undertaker. I've known him since he were a lad and he'll do a good job. I fancy a set of his brass handles on an oak coffin."

"Esther, Esther — stop talking so daft. He'll make the lasses a washing tub afore he does that," Thom chided.

She hushed him into silence. "I know what I'm saying. I want Salvation Army to bury me. They're always a lot more cheerful about do's like that and I want to them to sing '*The well is deep and I require the drops of the water of life.*' I've never forgotten you singing that Thom, when we were first wed. And you know that nice spot, right near the arches on path edge, where we used to sit when we took the bairns for a walk, I want that plot for you and me, lad. It's a grand little spot. It's sunny and I quite fancy me and thee resting there."

There was nothing any of them could say, and seeing their discomfort she turned to Thom and asked him to sing one of her favourite hymns, '*When the roll is called up yonder.*'

Some divine spirit guided them through the words and melody. Ada thought it was a bad dream, a Victorian melodrama that would soon end, but in her heart she knew her Mam meant every word and although her every instinct was to run away she stayed at the bedside.

"I'm not afraid, Thom. I'm ready to answer the call. In fact, I'm quite looking forward to a nice long sleep. But you — now you take care of yoursen and do as the lasses tell you."

She barely finished the sentence and then fell back on the pillow into a deep sleep — at least that's what Thom thought. The lasses knew that Mam was unconscious. Thom pulled the covers up to her neck and signalled them to go out.

"By hek, I could do with a cup of tea and no mistake. Esther does take on sometimes," he said.

They busied themselves with the tea and then Ada beckoned Aggie to follow her upstairs. "I reckon Mam's unconscious, but don't say owt to Dad yet," she whispered, but as she pushed open the bedroom door she knew Mam's life was over — she had passed into the morning.

36

From then on, things happened in a blur, a rushed cloud of letting everyone know — the undertaker, the Salvation Army, preparing the funeral tea. On the outside Thom appeared calm but Ada knew her Dad and could feel his broken heart.

"I never reckoned hearts could break, but I reckon Mam's dying has done mine in," Aggie said.

"Oh, hearts don't really break, Aggie. They bend a bit, but they don't break. I know, believe me. Give it time."

"It's not the same for you, Ada. I never had anybody but Mam and Dad. You had Wilf and that. All I've known is this house and work and Mam and Dad."

"Aye, and sometimes I reckon I would have been better off without it all," Ada mused.

After the hue and cry of the funeral, which set a gloom over St. John's Street, they settled down into a routine with Ada taking on the role of organiser — the foreman again. They kept Thom occupied with little jobs, for which he was grateful. It helped him forget for a while and also made him feel wanted and useful.

Polly had come down to help with the funeral and she and Ada got on to the old familiar footing. Ada visited two or three times a week and would bring her down for Sunday tea. It was a bit of company for Dad and they would chat away about the good old days.

But only a short month after Esther had died, Polly's neighbour, Dotty Wilson, came running down to fetch Ada.

"Polly's had a right funny turn, Ada, trembling like a jelly she is," she said.

Dear God, not more, Ada thought to herself as she hurried up to the house. "See to things here, Aggie. I'll get back as fast as I can," she said.

Polly was laid down on the couch and Dotty and Ada managed to get her upstairs before the doctor arrived.

"Well Ada, you do seem to be getting it lately. I'm afraid Mrs. Tanner is not going to get over this. She's had a massive seizure and I'll be very surprised if she lasts through the night. Can you stay with her?" he asked.

"Aye, aye, I'll stay. I'll send for Gertie and hope she gets here in time."

She wired for Gertie and then settled herself down for the night's vigil. Occasionally the old girl would call out and Ada would wet her lips and make her comfortable. She rallied towards the morning and told Ada what a good lass she was.

"And I've wronged you so many times lass. But now, I'll make up for it. I've a tidy bit in insurance. Mr. Allison knows all about it and it's for you and Gertie. When all is paid out there'll be still be a tidy sum left. Tell Gertie for me, won't you? And tell her to find herself a nice bloke and get wed, aye?" She smiled and then fell asleep.

In the early hours of the morning she died quite peacefully and Ada was surprised to find herself weeping bitterly.

Gertie arrived home in the midst of the tears and tried to comfort her. "Get it out of your system Ada. God knows we've both had a plateful."

Ada and Gertie followed Polly's coffin, walking arm in arm, holding on to each other for support.

Throughout that week they cleared the house. The few possessions they gave away to neighbours, keeping only a photograph each of the lads when they were little.

"What's it all been for, Gertie, just tell me for what?"

"Don't ask me, lass. It's too deep for me. But, do you know Ada, in a way I feel a great sense of relief, as if now the past is all behind me and I can start afresh. Do you understand?"

Ada nodded. She did, in a way. All ties with the past were broken. Now there was only the future.

The amount Polly left when all was paid out was a surprising three hundred pounds — and half each was a tidy sum. She'd not spent much of late for Ada had seen to most of the finances. The pension she received for Harry had steadily mounted up and, with the insurance, Polly was far richer in death than she had ever been in life.

Ada and Gertie parted emotionally, with promises to meet often. "We mustn't lose touch Ada, not after what we've shared," Gertie said as she boarded the train.

"You're set up nicely now, our Ada," Aggie later said when she was told about Polly's money. "What are you planning on doing with it all?"

"I'm going to expand the laundry. I'm going to see if Neil Simmons will let us have that warehouse next door that he doesn't use and then I'm taking on a couple of girls — Lily Hartley for one — and then I'll put the steam laundry out of business."

Aggie laughed at her sister, but she knew that Ada had never forgotten or forgiven Mrs. Price for treating her the way she had done.

"Retribution will be mine sayeth the Lord, aye?" Aggie laughed.

"No — sayeth Ada Tanner."

Polly, the last person in the world she would have dreamt of, had opened another door — the door she intended to be marked 'success.'

CHAPTER SIX

After going fully into the aspects of becoming tenants and landlord, Neil Simmons and Ada struck a bargain that suited them both. He was glad of the extra cash it would bring in, and as the whole country was now beginning to feel the edge of the depression, he had found more often than not the warehouse in question had been half empty most of the time. Folk weren't buying as much these days.

It was a huge building and though it stood only over the wall from where the girls worked, the access was only through Neil's big double doored back entrance. They talked of making a way straight through from the house yard, but after advice from Ralph, Ada decided not to. It would be too costly, and if the venture didn't pay off — well, she didn't fancy losing brass at this stage. That would give folk too much to talk about.

"Why not keep this washhouse at home for the hand and fine stuff, which I can do and still see to things in the house, and have the bigger stuff over at the warehouse?" Aggie suggested.

It struck Ada as a good idea. She could still keep the books at home and with extra hands could keep an eye on both places. She was amazed at how she had learned mistrust — especially of workers and tradesmen.

"I never would have thought it, our Aggie, but I'm a damn sight worse that Mrs. Price. I'm getting so that I don't trust anybody. And I shouldn't you know, 'cos, in spite of everything, God's been good in a lot of ways."

"Well, I'm damned. I never thought I'd hear you say owt like that. Things must be looking up," Aggie laughed, relieved that now perhaps some of the heavy weight of sadness would lift.

First they went to see Lily Hartley and asked her to work for them. Ada knew what she was doing, for Lily was utterly trustworthy and as strong as a horse.

"I don't want to do owt underhand Lil, like take you away from steam laundry if you don't want to. But there's a job for you with me if you want it, and a bit more brass in your hand each week and all."

She took the job, but Lily also knew Ada, and was fully aware that she would more than earn it.

Word got round that they needed a washerwoman and they had scores of applications, for both Ada and Aggie were well respected and known for being fair and honest. Ada kept holding back. She didn't know why, but something seemed to tell her to wait.

"Ada, did you know that Molly Drayton has had a little lad. He is a few months old now and a right bonny one. Yon Billy Acton buggered off and left her though. Crafty devil pays half-a-crown a week for the lad, and she had to summons him to get that — at least her Mam did."

"Aye, she would," Ada thought to herself, but she sensed that Lily was up to something, half-guessing the reason for the flow of information.

"Is she working then?" Ada asked, trying to sound casual.

"Nay, Missus wouldn't take her back after the accident and especially with Billy still being on the vans. Poor lass is a bit hard-pushed and whatever she's done, or is, she's a damned good worker."

Ada made nothing of it, but later on in the day as she went to the bank in the High Street she called in at the Drayton's cottage.

Molly was surprised at the visit, but not as unwelcoming as she had been on the last visit.

"Now then Molly, where's this bairn of yours?" Ada asked a startled Molly.

"He's in the drawer upstairs, asleep I hope. In spite of the money you gave us I couldn't run to a proper cot. We took one of the big drawers out for him. It's big enough for now."

She stood looking a bit helpless, as if not knowing what Ada wanted her to do next.

"Well, bring him down and let's tek a look."

"You've not come to give charity again have you, Ada? I don't want that. Things are a bit of a struggle, but I'm managing."

"No, you aren't, you know damn well. And I haven't come to offer charity. I'm not an institution. I've come to offer you a job."

"A job — where — and what the hell could I do with a bairn at my apron strings?"

"Job's in my laundry as washerwoman. You can bring bairn down with you and we'd tuck him in one of the wooden tubs. He'd be as snug as a bug and when he starts running about, well, then we'll think again."

"God, Ada, you are a one. After all that's happened. Eh, fancy you doing this for me."

"Well, as I've told Lily, you'll work for your brass. I'll not do you

41

any favours that way. But if a quid a week will help, then that's what I'm offering."

A quid was wealth indeed and Molly knew it to be above the usual wage. Like Lily, she also knew the money would be well earned. Ada was no slavedriver, but she never stood for slacking.

"Well?" Ada was getting impatient. Doing a good turn was one thing, but she wasn't going to waste any more time.

"Who the hell could refuse that, Ada? I'll be there first thing on Monday morning."

"If you're taking job, you'll be there first thing tomorrow morning — seven sharp."

And, bright and sharp, Molly presented herself for work, fulfilling Ada's faith in her being a good worker. At first they put the baby in the washhouse and then Thom strolled through and the next thing he was in the house with him. But this move on Ada's part started a friendship that was to last a lifetime.

The face of the town began to change. All along the front new sea walls and the esplanade were being built. More and more people were finding that Brid was indeed bright and breezy. They had to be catered for. The new building work also gave the boarding houses a rise in economy for throughout the winter months they were full of lodgers from the gangs of workers. They were a mixed bunch drawn by the lure of work from all over the country.

The High Street boarding houses were also experiencing a boom, and all of this in turn reflected upon Ada's business, which now needed more hands to cope with all the work.

Molly was put in charge of the washhouse with another married woman and a young girl working with her. She proved more than her worth and Ada often sighed as she thought of her wasted life. Aggie coped with all the church and fine stuff and Lily and Cissie ironed and pressed.

Ada — well, Ada kept her finger in all the pies, filling in wherever needed, but most of her time was in administration. It was a very busy group and although she laughed when Ada talked of taking over the steam laundry, Aggie hoped that they would stay a small family concern.

"I reckon I've got a couple of millionaires in the family," Thom would say to his son Bert. "It's a pity you ain't got a bit more about you like our Ada." He was very proud of her business-like manner and wished many times that she had been a lad. "I'd have put her in Parliament, that I would," he would say, absolutely convinced that she would have risen to be Prime Minister.

One or two of the men employed on the sea front would bring down their washing and stay to chat with the women, and Thom too, if he happened to be around.

With work being so good, it was decided to have a young girl in the house to see to the meals and cleaning and also Molly's boy, who, so far, had not been given a name. He was referred to as 'the bairn.'

Thom would walk with the boy through the yard and sometimes into the washhouse. The men would play for a moment or two, and one took to bringing down the odd goodie or so.

He was a tall, thin bloke with black, straight hair. Ada thought him a nice respectable sort and took to hanging around for a chat. She had been so busy with building up the business that she had forgotten what it was like to talk to a bloke and to see the appreciation in his eyes as he looked her up and down.

"Don't tell me you fancy him, not after all these years on your own?" Aggie teased.

Ada was now well into her thirties. "You can just stop that. He's just a nice bloke. Anyroad, he's too young for me. I'd be cradle snatching."

His name was Cyril Clamp and he was twenty-eight, not a bit like Wilf in looks or in manner and Ada thought that was the reason she had taken to him. Remembering her love for Wilf was still painful, but life had to go on.

She started going to the bank at twelve, hoping that she would catch Cyril on his way home to dinner. They would walk, side by side, talking about everyday things, like the weather and work. He never offered to suggest a meeting or once stepped out of place. He talked of the parents who had split up, how he had been sent into the army at fourteen along with his brothers and how, down south where he came from, there wasn't any work. He had been told to try Hull and had been labouring for a while there when someone mentioned the Brid sea walls. He had got there and found it to be a very pleasant place.

"I like it here 'cos everybody's friendly. I reckon I'm going to see if I can get my old man a job here. He's been having a rough time of it lately."

Evidently his father was a blacksmith, but there seemed to be some cloud when his name was mentioned.

"Is he a good blacky?" Ada asked.

Cyril nodded and she suggested that he ask at Forbes, the smithy further down St. John Street.

"I heard they needed another hand," she said.

After that conversation she did not see him for a few days and began to wonder if he had gone away. One dinner time she looked up to see him coming round the corner of St. John Street and High Street. But she did not wave or acknowledge him. Better not let him think she was chasing after him. Her name was called out and she turned to wait until he caught up with her.

"You move fast for a little 'un. I want to thank you for saying about Forbes. They want to see my Dad and he's coming up next week. I've been down to Spalding to see him for a few days."

She smiled and said how nice.

"If he gets the job will you let us take you out as a thank you?" he asked.

She made nothing of this, telling him not to count his chickens before they hatched. But, secretly, she hoped his Dad would get the job for she quite fancied a night out with a man for a change. These days it was always her and Aggie.

Work had become her life and now the thought of the future holding piles of washing was beginning to pall a little. She didn't quite fancy Aggie and herself living together like two old maids, in spite of the fact they were getting on so well together. She decided not to exactly be on the look out, but to, well, keep her options open.

She was always glad when Saturday afternoon came round. It meant a rest and the chance of some fresh air — weather permitting.

She and Aggie were discussing over fish and chips whether or not to go to Hull for a bit of shopping when the heavy knocker on the front door bellowed through the house. Ada sighed and went to answer it to find Cyril and another man at his side, stood on the doorstep.

"Dad got that job and as I said, we've come to ask you out to say thanks. And have you got a friend to bring so that we won't be odd numbers?"

She turned and looked at the man standing there. This must be another brother, he looked so like Cyril and about three or four years older. He was tall and thin — very thin. His face was gaunt and

44

his nose looked as if it had been bent. His eyes — they were the most startling blue she had ever seen — steely blue and so expressionless that they sent a shiver down her back.

Cyril noticed her looking and said, "Oh, by the way, this is my Dad."

"Dad? He doesn't look old enough, " she gasped.

"Well, I am, miss. Cyril here is my oldest lad." He smiled at her, but the smile never quite reached his eyes. He was smart — a navy pin-striped suit, white shirt and a checked cap jauntily set on the side of his head. Over his right arm he carried a gaberdine raincoat folded and buttoned correctly so that it did not crease.

What it was about him, she could not say. Taken one at a time his features were anything but good and yet set in that bone structure they gave the impression of being handsome. And there was something, something about him that drew her. She felt his amusement at her obvious interest.

"You must have had monkey glands then," she laughed to hide her feelings.

"Not exactly. But I can still hold my own with these young 'uns," he answered.

And again, the look in his eyes and his soft Suffolk burr sent a spine-tingling thrill through her body. By hell, this was a rare bloke and no mistake.

Again he smiled and Cyril coughed as if to remind her of the purpose of the visit.

"Hang on a minute and I'll see if our Aggie will come with us. If she comes then I'll come, but I'll not come on me own."

"Don't worry miss, I shan't eat you," Cyril's father joked.

"And we'd best get one thing straight. I'm missus not miss — a widow mind you, but still missus."

"Oh pardon me." He spoke sarcastically and taking off his cap made a mocking, sweeping bow.

By this time, Aggie had come to the door to see what was going on and after a nudge or two from Ada agreed to go out on the foursome. The meeting place was to be the Picture Palace at six o'clock.

The two men left with a wave and a smile, Cyril clearly pleased that he had pulled off a meeting. Aggie, well, she was not so pleased. Well, pleased maybe, but somewhat nervous.

"I've never been out with a fellow in my life, our Ada. What the devil made you do that? I must say though, that bloke is a fine figure of a man," she chatted to Ada as they got ready to go out.

Ada looked across and caught the slightest hint of interest in her sister's face. "By hek," she thought, Aggie felt the attraction, too. Well, they would see what the night brought.

A few minutes before six that night they were walking towards the Picture Palace seeing, as they approached, the two men standing waiting.

"He's not bad is he, Ada — his Dad, I mean. I can't believe he's old enough. I'm quite looking forward to tonight. Older men always make me feel more comfortable."

Ada looked at her reflection in a shop window. She didn't look bad either, for an old 'un. Her donkey brown velvet trimmed suit and cream silk blouse made a good match for her skin, handbag and shoes. No, she didn't look bad at all. And may the best man win, she thought to herself.

Upon meeting, both men proferred boxes of chocolates. Ada held back for a minute to see what Aggie would do. She rushed forward and took those from Cyril's Dad. Well, let her get on with it. If Ada was right, he wouldn't take anyone who was too forward.

She turned and as she took the box from Cyril she asked, "What is your Dad's name, you never told us?"

"Oh — I'm sorry — it's Rob — Rob Clamp."

"Um — Rob Clamp, eh? Well, it's not such a bad mug to put handle on," she laughed.

His eyes flickered with interest as she spoke, but Aggie took his arm saying, "Shall we get on then or we'll miss the big picture?"

As he turned to follow, Ada could have sworn his eyelid dropped in a wink, but it happened so quickly he could well have been just blinking.

The picture was funny — daft, Rob said — Charlie Chaplin up to his capers and making them laugh. Aggie laughed heartily at every antic. Ada, well she laughed at the really funny parts. She didn't want to sound like a daft schoolgirl. It was easy to see Aggie had not enjoyed much of men's company.

As they filed out of the pictures into the twilight, Rob asked if they would like to go for a drink.

"In a pub, you mean? Not likely. I've never been in a pub in my life and I'm not starting now. We aren't that sort, are we Ada?" Aggie spoke quickly.

Ada frowned, thinking to herself, "Well, you might not be, but I'm old enough to try anything once."

Sensing the uneasiness, Rob suggested that they would take a walk along the front.

Ada had never known Aggie be so pushing. As they walked she made sure that she was near Rob. If he so much as moved a step she was either at his side or just enough in front to make sure Ada couldn't get a look in. Well, let her, Ada reckoned. There was plenty of time to alter things if need be.

The foursome became quite regular, and with no signs of any definite pairing off. Rob was politeness itself and took an equal interest in both girls, but Ada always felt there was an extra flicker of interest whenever their eyes met.

It surprised her one Saturday night when Aggie came down ready to go out on the usual date wearing a new navy blue dress and matching coat. She'd not said a word about it to Ada, who could see it was tailor made, one of Sally Ripley's handiwork. By hell, she must be smitten.

"You kept that quiet, our lass. What's on, then?" she asked casually.

Aggie blushed as she answered. "Well, Rob is always paying me little compliments and, well, that sort of thing makes you want to make a special effort like." She smiled coyly at Ada.

So it was war was it? Hmmn, thought Ada, we'll soon settle your hash.

It was the custom during the interval to have ice creams and as Cyril passed them down the row Ada tipped her elbow and knocked two of them over, conveniently near enough to slither right down the front of Aggie's new outfit. She apologised profusely and tried to help clean the mess, making damn sure that as she did she rubbed it right into the weave of the material. It looked absolutely awful.

"You clumsy devil. I'll have to go home and change now," said Aggie. "Are you coming with me?" she snapped at Ada.

"No, that would be rude to leave the fellows. You run on and we'll walk up slow to meet you." The answer was ready and pat.

CHAPTER SEVEN

Aggie left in a fury and Ada gave no sign that the whole incident was anything but an accident. But once outside the pictures she made no bones about who she was going to walk with.

She took Rob's arm firmly and turning to Cyril said, "You go on up and fetch Aggie. We'll meet you at the corner of the Promenade in about twenty minutes."

Cyril looked hard at them both. This was not the way he had thought things to be. He could see from Ada's look that his presence was not required.

Rob never spoke a word as if, almost, it was nothing to do with him. However, he made no move to take his arm away as he and Ada walked down the street in silence.

"That was a crafty move, my girl. Do you reckon on being as forward with men as that?" he eventually asked.

"Not really. To tell you the truth, I've not bothered with fellows since Wilf was killed. But I reckon I know what I want and I usually get it." Her answer came without any hesitation, and she could hardly believe it was herself she could hear saying these things. Fancy Ada Tanner making up to a bloke like that.

Wilf would never have believed it of her, but somehow this man was different. He magnetised her into doing and saying things she would not normally dream of. He thrilled her too, as no man ever had — not even Wilf. The very touch of his arm sent shivers down her spine.

"I've noticed one thing about you, Rob. You never seem to smile properly. Your mouth might move, but the smile never reaches your eyes," she said.

"I've not had much in my life to smile about," he answered.

She loved his brogue, a really southern brogue which he had never lost in all the years he had been away from Suffolk.

"I don't know as I have either, for that matter," she replied and then to her amazement found herself telling him all about Wilf — even Billy Acton and Molly. She couldn't think why she was doing it. What the hell would he want to know all that muck for? She'd never talked this way not to anyone, but she couldn't stop herself.

He listened quietly, making no comment except to tell her she shouldn't have been so daft about Billy Acton. "You should never lead a bloke on unless you mean business — not ever," he said.

"Well, I shan't again. Next time I'll mean it." Good God, she was off again.

After a little pressure Rob started to tell her how he had got to Brid by walking from Hull, how during the past few months he had walked most of the country in search of work. Sometimes he had found lodgings for a few coppers and sometimes he had slept rough.

"Do you know, Ada, one night I slept in a doss house on a clothes line for a penny and I was that fagged out I slept right through the night."

"By hek, that was a bit rough. But what about your wife, Cyril's Mam, what about her?"

He went coldly quiet, but passed off the question lightly without really saying anything at all.

They heard a voice calling out their names and turning saw Cyril running towards them by himself. Aggie was so mad she had decided not to join them again.

"Oh well, I suppose I'd best get off home too," she said and then was pleasantly surprised to hear Rob tell his son to go on up to the Black Horse where he would meet him later.

"Have you got to go in just yet? Can't we walk down the Forty Foot and round that way?" he asked.

Ada decided to throw all caution to the wind and agree. They walked slowly, talking about things in a comfortably companionable way until Ada saw that they were almost at Sewerby. She didn't want that. No, that would be awful, to walk with this stranger where she and Wilf had shared so many memories. And what would George and Isabella say if they happened to meet them?

"I've got a sister lives in that big house, the hall," she said.

"In service is she then?" he asked.

Ada just answered no, deciding not to say anything about Isabella. That might sound like bragging and put him off, just when things were going nicely.

"I'll have to be getting home now, but I've enjoyed this walk and the talk," she smiled.

"Shall we go out alone next week?" he asked.

"Yes — yes if you like. It will be a nice change."

The path became uneven and she stumbled over a cobble, banging her face against his shoulder. With one swift movement he turned and took hold of her shoulders and kissed her with an intense passion that she had never before experienced.

She answered with her whole being. Dear God, what was this feeling that was tearing through her body? She tingled, she shook and trembled, cold one minute hot the next. No man — not even Wilf — had stirred such passion within her.

At last he let her go and looked down into her eyes. "Till next week then?" he said.

She nodded, not daring to allow herself to say anything. They then walked briskly home where she found Aggie waiting for her.

"You bitch — you bloody bitch — you did that on purpose to get rid on me," she shouted in temper.

Ada had never seen her sister so roused. Hek, she must really have got it bad for Rob. But all was fair in love and war.

"I saw him bring you home. You meant to get him on your own didn't you?" She rushed over to Ada in a frenzy and smacked her hard across her face.

Ada stumbled, but quickly recovered and grabbing Aggie's arm twisted it behind her back so hard that she yelled out in pain and surprise.

The cry awoke Thom, who came downstairs to see what was going on. He couldn't believe his eyes when he saw his two grown-up daughters fighting like a couple of school kids.

"What the hell's this about?" he asked and amid angry sobs Aggie gave her version of what had happened.

The trouble was, most of her story was the truth and so Ada kept silent and just shrugged her shoulders.

"You mean to tell me you're fighting over a feller? Well, what would your Mam think to that? She'll be turning in her grave. If this is it, we'll not have any fellers here again. I'm not having my house made like this for a man. You both ought to have more pride in yoursens." Thom was hurt and angry at his daughters.

"She had the same chance as me, Dad. She should have gone after him if she had wanted him that much," Ada said in some sort of defence.

"That's enough of that, my lass. And remember, he's not to come here, not even to the door."

Her Dad was really angry now, but she didn't care. She'd still see Rob. If any man could make her feel like he did then it was worth putting up with a bit of bother.

"If I want to see him, then I shall. I don't give a damn if he doesn't come here, but I shall see him. I'll meet him if I want to," she

50

declared and then marched up to her room leaving behind an alien and icy atmosphere.

During the following weeks it seemed that the whole family had turned against her. Aggie had taken the whole affair so badly that she had gone the rounds of the family telling them — with great embellishment — her version of the story.

It hurt Ada that, with the exception of Isabella, not one of them came to ask her what had happened. "Surely you must know that whatever I might be I don't tell yarns. I'd tell them the truth." But her past, as they called it, was against her and with all the gossip you'd have thought she was man mad.

"I know you, Ada, what has really been going on, and who is this ruddy bloke?" Isabella asked.

Ada told her briefly what had happened.

"And are you that keen on him?"

"To tell you the truth, I don't really know now. With all that's gone on, I'm fair muddled. I don't know what to say."

"Well, I'll say this then, if ever you want a few days out of the way — then you know where we are. As I see it I have no right to judge you or anybody else and God knows you've been through enough."

Ada swallowed hard to hide the tears. "Thanks, our Bella." She used the childhood name her sister had been known by.

"How's Dad taking it? I'm glad for one thing, Mam's not here to see it all."

"He's not bad. I don't reckon poor old lad knows who to believe, and as for Mam, well I wish she was here. By hell, she'd have put everybody straight and no messing."

"This man, Rob whatever his name is, would Mam have liked him?"

Ada sighed and thought for a while before answering. Truth was she didn't rightly know what Mam would have thought for Rob wasn't like anyone she'd ever met before. Maybe that was his attraction — the unknown quantity.

"All I can say Isabella, is that if me and our Aggie are both gone on him then there must be summat."

"Aye, maybe. But is it the right summat? I never thought our Aggie would go on like this about a bloke. And I'm not saying she's in the wrong mind you. But, well, I can understand a bit. I know during the war when George was away for years, and when he came

51

back in such a state, well I yearned to be — loved — you know what I mean. Is that the attraction — is it in 'that way'?"

, Ada smiled now. It had taken a lot for Isabella to talk in this way. Loving or anything of that sort was not a subject women normally talked about.

"Well, I've missed Wilf — in 'that way' as you put it — and no mistake. Eh, the night's I've laid there longing for his arms to enfold me, to feel his flesh against mne." She paused and looked at her sister. "Does that shock you?"

Isabella shook her head. "Not really. I know the feeling only too well. But that's not something our Aggie would know about, is it? He must have something else."

"I reckon it's because he's very much his own man — a real man. I know this, he makes my toes curl, and I feel a sense of belonging to him. I loved Wilf, you know that. But Rob, well it is something very different. I don't know how else to put it."

"Oh I reckon I know what you mean, lass, and though I'm not taking sides, remember what I said — and don't go upsetting our Dad too much. He should be having peace and quiet at his time of life."

"That's expecting a bit with our lot, isn't it?" Ada laughed, feeling better now that she had if not an ally, then a support in her sister.

She'd never given a thought to Isabella and George, thinking that with all their brass and the set up they'd got, they must be all right. But what about their personal life? Poor old Georgie can't have been much good when he first came home. God, how selfish and thoughtless can you get when you're wrapped up in your own problems. Bella must have gone through a bit and all. Seems I'm not the only one, Ada mused to herself.

Aggie seemed to go a bit mental and wouldn't even sit at the table to eat her meals with Ada, either waiting until she had finished or started before her. Ada decided to ignore it all and calmly tried to carry on as if nothing was amiss.

At work she would address Aggie, who would reply either through Molly or Lily. It caused a few laughs until during one long conversation which involved both of the women Lily lost her temper.

"Bloody hell — isn't it time all this daftness stopped? You're like a couple of bitches on heat. That bloody bloke must be something for

52

you two to carry on like this. I've a good mind to chuck a bucket of water over both of you. Maybe that will calm things down a bit."

That made Ada laugh, but Aggie — well, that incensed her mood more than ever. As Ada got ready to meet Rob that night Aggie sat staring at her with such concentration that it was eerie. If looks could have killed . . . Ada was pleased to get out of the house.

When she met Rob it had begun to drizzle with rain.

"Look, we can't walk about in this lot. How about coming for a drink? You needn't have anything but a lemonade. It's daft stopping out in this lot," Rob said.

She would have liked to have asked him home, but that was impossible. Oh well, she might as well be hung for a sheep as a lamb, she thought, and agreed to go for a drink.

When she entered the Ship Inn she could feel the atmosphere, the stares knifed her back — Ada Tanner in a pub! The landlord, Horace Sendler, whom Ada had known all her life, hardly spoke a civil word to either of them. Normally he was a genial man, always a laugh and a joke. It wasn't that he had any objection to Rob, more that he just did not want Ada to get mixed up with the kind of women who frequented his pub. Men — that was different — but no decent women went into pubs and in his book Ada was a decent woman. The atmosphere became so tense that Rob suggested they should leave.

"But where shall we go, it's pittling down now?" she asked.

"Come up to my lodgings. My landlady and her old man have gone off to the pictures. Anyway, they won't say anything."

"On our own you mean?" she gasped.

"Well, I've told you before, I shan't eat you," he laughed.

It was pouring in torrents as they left the Ship Inn and Rob grabbed her hand in his and started to run the few yards to his lodgings. Once inside the door they stopped for breath and he put his arms around her and laughed into her face.

"You can shift if you have to," he smiled.

She wriggled from his grasp. "Don't hold me like that or I'll be all creased. I'm wet through."

"Take your clothes off and let them dry. There's a good fire here in the kitchen, we can soon dry off."

She hesitated and thought to herself, oh sod it, nothing can happen unless I want it to. Rob wasn't the sort to force himself on a

53

woman. She followed him into the warm room where she found he had already begun to undress.

"Come on, get near the fire and warm yourself. Here, give me your coat." He took her coat from her shoulders.

Slowly she undressed — first her dress, then her shoes and finally her stockings. She left on her crêpe de chine camisole and stood with her back to Rob, not quite knowing what to do next. No man had ever seen her undress, only Wilf, and she felt awkward and shy.

Rob went to her and without any preliminaries kissed her, fondling her tiny breasts as his lips covered hers.

"You're quite a lady, Ada, quite a lady. I could take to you in no uncertain way." He spoke between kisses that he poured on her lips. She responded in a way that she had never thought herself capable of, and made no resistance when he gently pushed her down on to the pegged hearth rug in front of the fire.

She knew what was about to happen and she could not, indeed, did not, want to stop it. "I've never done owt like this before, not since I was wed," she tried to say between his passionate kisses and the thrusting of his body into hers.

She was giving herself to him, moving with his movements until the passion within her was released and she screamed with ecstasy and pain.

When it was all over they lay still and quietly. "I'm not a loose woman, you know. You're the only man that's touched me, apart from Wilf."

"I can tell that, Ada. But it was good, wasn't it?"

"I've never experienced anything like it before — not even with Wilf — it was . . .," her voice tailed off in shyness for she knew not how to express the feelings that burned through her body.

Rob appeared not to notice her hesitant shyness now that the flush of passion had subsided. Calmly he made them a cup of tea and then handed her her clothes, almost dry, but still with a hint of dampness and mustiness about them.

Swiftly she dressed for it was now getting quite late, and some inexplicable reasoning within her was urging her to get home, to get away. It was not that she wanted to leave Rob, far from it. But her emotions were becoming claustrophobic and she desperately needed to be on her own to try and sort out the feelings and emotions that surged inside her.

The words that passed between them were of everyday inconse-

54

quences. He walked her down the street and she felt that every eye was on her, that everyone knew what had happened between her and this man, an almost comparative stranger.

Just before they reached the old house she stopped and held up her arm. "Don't bother to come any further," she said. "Our Aggie has got herself a bit upset about us. Best not to let her see us together — eh?"

She tried to make light of her words but could see that Rob was not fooled. He knew exactly what had been going on.

"But you're not going to let it make any difference to us are you, Ada? You've no regrets about what we did — about tonight?" he asked.

Ada shook her head. "No Rob. I'm not the type to be sorry. I'm not sorry one bit, love." And leaning forward on tiptoe, she kissed him tenderly as they parted.

CHAPTER EIGHT

Quietly, she let herself into the dusky gloom of the house, answering her Dad's call of, "Is that you Ada?" with a soft, "Yes, Dad, I'll come in and see you in a minute." She crept upstairs pausing on the landing to notice that Aggie's door was slightly open. So she'd been waiting had she. Well, to hell with her. She could whistle if she thought about starting a row tonight.

"We got caught in that storm, Dad, and had to shelter. That's why I'm late." She spoke as she popped her head around Thom's bedroom door and then smiled as she heard the regular breathing of his sleep. It still made her heart ache when she saw her Mam's empty pillow laid down Thom's back so that the great bed did not feel so empty for him. Ah well, no good brooding, not tonight of all nights. Tonight she had a lot of thinking to do. How was she going to face Aggie for one thing? She never missed owt. Ada felt sure she would guess what they'd been up to.

But in the morning nothing was said. Instead, Aggie treated Ada to a hostile silence which became so bad that after a few days whenever Ada entered a room Aggie would get up and walk out. Ada tried to talk to her sister, to explain that no-one can dictate to their feelings, that she understood that Aggie must be feeling grim because Rob preferred her. But it was to no avail and they finally fell into a silent world, speaking only when it concerned work.

And, in spite of their personal quarrel, the laundry work continued to prosper. Work poured in and Aggie continued to pull her weight. But after a few weeks the atmosphere became unbearable. Ada could feel Aggie's eyes boring into her and if they faced each other she could see the venom in her eyes.

They tried to keep it all from Thom, but when Ada stopped going into the house for the morning break he began to sense that something was amiss with his lasses. Ada tried the excuse that the girls took too long a break if no-one was there to keep an eye on them, but Thom was no fool. In spite of his age, he knew whatever was wrong was to do with that fellow. Now he wished he had not forbidden Ada to take him to the house. It might have given him a chance to size the bloke up and maybe learn what was causing all this bother. Still, neither of his lasses were bairns any longer. They would have to work things out for themselves. But oh, if only his Esther were here, she would sort them out in no time. He didn't like all this bitterness in the family. There had never been anything like this before and he was too old to deal with it now.

Molly had watched the situation getting worse and her heart ached for both of them, especially for Ada, who seemed to be going from one thing to another these days.

"You know, Ada, things would be a damn sight better if you stopped seeing that Rob Clamp," she told her as they sat over their morning tea.

Ada thought a few minutes before answering. "Molly, I could no more stop seeing Rob than I could stop the moon rising."

Molly stared at her. "As bad as that is it then?"

Ada nodded and sighed.

"Well, I'm sorry for your Aggie like, with her never having a bloke. But, well, I'm your mate and if ever I can do owt, well, you know, Ada."

Molly touched Ada's arm and the feel of the comforting hand brought tears to her eyes.

"I can't see that my having Rob will make all that much difference to our Aggie. It's not as if I took him from her, Molly. He never wanted her in the first place." She swallowed hard to keep back the tears.

"Now come on, Ada, be fair. Poor old Aggie's never fancied a bloke before, not one, and then when she does he prefers her sister — and one that's been married before and all. She really does fancy Clamp you know, and you think about it, if you wed him whilst you're still in partnership, she could have a hell of a lot to lose."

Molly looked Ada straight in the face as she spoke. Ada frowned. 'Molly — Molly — tell me something — and be honest. You don't like Rob do you? Now come on, spit it out."

Now Molly sighed — wanting to continue the honest friendship and yet not wanting to hurt Ada who had been her only friend when she needed one so badly. "Well, love, I don't honestly know the bloke, but there's just something about him. I can't put my finger on it, but there's just something that's not quite right about him. Eh, I don't know."

"And not so much about getting wed either. I've honestly never thought that far Molly. I'm getting a bit long in the tooth for that, and so is he for that matter — he's eleven years older than me. Unless I have to get wed of course and there's not much chance of that even at my age." She laughed as she spoke more to cover the embarrassment when she realised what she had said than anything else.

Molly was a bit too quick on the uptake and gave her an old-fashioned look. "Blimey, Ada, you're not playing daft games like that are you? I thought I was the only one that did things like that. And you just remember, there's many a slip — by hell you're a deep one and no mistake."

They laughed together — Molly in surprise and Ada in relief that she had been able to talk to someone at last.

"No. I'm only teasing, Molly," she said.

"Teasing or not my lass, I reckon that Clamp bloke has more hold over you than I thought. There's a lot of talk about him, Ada. He likes his beer and he chats the women up a bit. A hell of a temper and all when he's aroused. I heard that he sent Reg Willows flying through the Star of Hope's glass doors the other night and just because . . ." she stopped in mid-flow.

Ada knew there was more to this and told her to carry on. "Spit it out, Molly. Why did he do it?"

"Well you know what old Reg is like — smell of a brewer's pinny. He said that Rob was getting his feet under the table, and two women to play with, bread buttered on both sides like. He doesn't know what he's saying though. Still, he got a fractured arm for his trouble."

"He's fine with me, Molly. I can only speak as I find," Ada quickly defended Rob.

"Well remember what I said, lass. I'm here if you ever need me."

The conversation stopped as Aggie entered the washhouse, lips pursed and expression set like thunder.

The weekly meetings increased to two or three times — Thursdays, Saturdays and Sundays. The weekends depended upon domino games, for Rob was in the league team and rated highly as a player.

As for the other nights, she never asked what he did with them. Somehow he did not welcome questions and as they enjoyed each other's company so much when they were together, she decided to let matters be. He never again asked her to go into a public house, but often they would go to his lodgings — not every week, but often enough to make their loving become a thrilling part of the relationship. Ada marvelled at the way she thrilled as on the first time, giving her an excitement that drove any thoughts of consequences out of her mind.

He told her a little about his past. She did learn that he had three sons by his first partner, a beautiful chorus girl from London who would not marry him. She asked what had happened to part them and Rob's face set in tight lines as he answered that the past was over and done with, no use dragging it all up. This satisfied Ada for she understood a little of how he felt. Her own brief past, her marriage with Wilf, now seemed like a distant dream that she preferred to leave that way. Far better to let things rest.

His strength impressed her. His tall, slender appearance and age belied the strength that would have credited a man half his age. His build reminded her of a piece of iron — hard and unbending. Suffering the worst years of the depression he had tramped the countryside looking for work and taking anything that came along.

"I've shovelled snow for a bob a day and one time I worked at Sheffield gas works non stop for three days — not an hour off — seventy two hours. That took some doing, but I was never out of work and always made enough money to keep myself. There was work if you were prepared to take it, and I was."

She admired him for that and was glad that he now had a steady job and seemed well set.

The rest of the family took care not to mention anything regarding the association. She knew damn well that Aggie had got in first and gone round giving her version. Ada had no intention of enlightening them at all. If they tried to venture the subject she gave them one of her looks — so like Esther's — and that soon put them off.

During the October she began to feel a bit out of sorts. She thought at first she must have picked up a bug and then maybe all this bother had brought back her billious attacks. Molly noticed the peaky looks and suggested that Ada see a doctor.

"I reckon I might do that, lass. I'm getting funny that I can't even enjoy a cup of tea these days."

Molly breathed in but said nothing except that she'd better get down to the surgery straight away and see what was wrong.

"It can't be much though, can it?" she asked.

Molly made out that she had not heard.

When Ada gave her symptoms to the doctor he bent forward and looked down at her over the top of his spectacles. "You couldn't be expecting could you, Ada? No, of course not. You're a widow aren't you? Not got a young man have you?"

Ada blushed. "Er — well I have sort of."

"But you haven't been doing anything to warrant a pregnancy have you — nothing silly at your age?"

Ada went beetroot red and Dr. Williams could see that he had stumbled on her secret.

"Well, my dear, well now, I'd have thought at your age you'd have known better. How old are you? Nearly forty — well, well, well."

"Oh it can't be that, doctor — not at my age — and I haven't done it all that many times — only once or twice — or so." Her voice began to rise, showing the panic inside her. Good God, what would she do if the doctor was right? A bairn, at her age. It would ruin the business — and Aggie — by hell she'd have a field day.

"Ada, Ada." She heard the doctor's voice break through her thoughts.

"You had better bring a specimen down first thing in the morning."

"A what — a specimen of what?"

The doctor stared. Really, how naïve could you get. Here she was having sex and no idea of the consequences. Patiently he told her the routine of taking a morning sample of water so that he could test it and either confirm or refute her suspected condition.

As she walked home her mind was in a turmoil. How the devil would she tell Rob? What would he say? Would he desert her like Billy Acton had done Molly — would he marry her — did she want to marry him? A thrill on the mat was one thing — a bairn and marriage — well, that was something entirely different. And what about Dad and the family?

Dear God, what had she been doing to let a thing like this happen. "Oh Mam, where are you, why aren't you here?" her heart cried out in anguish.

CHAPTER NINE

From the moment she got home she felt that Aggie's eyes were following her everywhere she went — in the kitchen, in the washhouse, in the pantry — everywhere, until Ada thought that she was going to follow her down the yard to the lavvy.

Getting an empty bottle, washing it out to take up to her room, developed into something that would have done credit to a spy thriller. The only bottle available was of cough mixture and it was half full. To empty it Ada made a false cough, taking two table-spoonfuls each time she pressed her throat to make it itch. Thom became very concerned, but Aggie just smirked.

"You ought to see a dcotor about that cough, our Ada. Don't let it get any worse. You don't want consumption do you now? I've not forgotten Johnny Sawden's wife dying of that," Thom said, and Ada could have kissed him for inadvertently he had given her the reason she needed to go down to the surgery openly without rousing any suspicions.

"I reckon I shall, Dad. I'll go down tomorrow night if we get done in time," she answered.

But getting the sample of water into the bottle was far more difficult than she had imagined. She thanked God that at least she had a room to herself and that night she carried the cough mixture bottle under her skirt and then hid it under her pillow. Oh, she was so sick of all this hide and seek. Why had she ever gone and got herself into such a mess?

She hardly slept and got up before she heard anyone else moving. Taking the big china jug from the washstand she used it to take the sample. That was fine, but trying to get it from the jug into the small neck of the bottle was another matter. Her hands shook and most of it went over the sides. What to do now? She crept downstairs and drank two cups of stone cold water in the hope that she would go again. Finally, after what seemed an eternity, she managed a depth of about half an inch in the bottom of the bottle.

"That'll have to do, bugger it. I can't do any more," she muttered, wrapping the bottle up in a large hankie and placing it inside one of her gloves.

At breakfast she pushed down a cup of tea and then made out she was going down the yard to the washhouse before it all came back again. She was thankful in a way that she and Aggie were not on

61

speaking terms. It saved her having to explain her odd behaviour, but it would have been nice to have someone to confide in, someone who might have a bit of understanding. Oh well, best get on with things. These thoughts ran through her mind making it spin until she could not contain herself.

"I'm going down to the doctor's this morning, Dad. I haven't slept all night with this cough. I can't keep taking that cough stuff any longer, it might be dangerous."

She heard Aggie grunt behind her back and it caught her on the raw. Any other time she would have ignored her, but now — now she felt so vulnerable, so frightened, and so alone. Thom saw her tremble as the tears rushed to her eyes.

"Aye, come on lass, don't take on. You're working too hard that's what it is, you know. Take it easy for a bit. No business is worth killing yourself for. Get off down to doctor's and tell him I said what you need is a good rest." He patted her shoulder and followed her down the passage to see that she put her coat and hat on.

"Poor Dad, if only he knew," she thought to herself.

Once in the surgery she calmed down a bit and welcomed the long wait to give herself time to think. Finally her name was called and she entered the room, praying that she was not expecting. But the prayers were to no avail for after testing the sample over the blue flame of the burner all hopes were dashed.

"I'm afraid the result is positive, Ada. You are pregnant. Did you really not have any idea at all? What about your periods, didn't you guess when they ceased?" the doctor asked.

"I've never been what you might call regular that way and I thought I might be on an early change like. There's no mistake then, I'm expecting?" she answered.

"No mistake at all, Ada." The answer was firm. "Now, I suggest that you go and tell this friend of yours and ask what he's going to do about it. Come and see me again in about two week's time and we'll try and find out how far the pregnancy is and get you a date to work on."

She had given no thought as to how she would take the news that she was about to become a mother and she certainly hadn't expected the feeling of calmness that came over her. It was as if a load had been lifted from her shoulders and she began to feel pangs of hunger rumbling inside her belly. By hek, she could eat a horse.

Without thinking, she made her way into the station cafe and ordered egg on toast with a cup of tea and ate the lot without feeling any pangs of sickness. Maybe it was the relief that had kept the food down, but now she had to face returning home her heart began to sink again.

Thom was waiting for her and she put him off by saying it was just a chill on the chest and stomach and he seemed satisfied. The one person she had to see was Rob. Until then she was keeping her mouth shut. The day dragged on and on. Aggie kept on giving her funny looks and smirking, but she was too worried and confused now to pay any attention to her.

Her thoughts were taken up by wondering how the hell she was going to tell Rob. They had not planned to meet tonight, but she would have to see him. There was no way she was going to suffer on her own any longer. He had to know how things were. Finally, common-sense took over and she decided that as he had had the same pleasure as herself then he must take the consequences. It takes two to make this kind of bargain and two to keep it.

Ada knew that she would find him in the bar of the Star, but wondered how to get in to speak to him. She would just have to be brazen and go in and get him. There was no time for buggering about — things had gone too far for that. At eight that night she put on her hat and coat, saying she was going for a walk. "There's somebody I want to see," she added, ignoring Aggie's "And we all know who that is."

Her brave spirit deserted her as she reached the double doors of the Star. It just wasn't done to go in there, not for Ada's sort of lass anyway. Thankfully she saw Ted Hardacre walking towards her. He would be going inside.

"Ted, will you ask Rob Clamp if I could have a word with him please. It is a bit urgent," she said.

"Fetch a bloke out of a pub, Ada? Now, that's coming it a bit, isn't it? But aye, lass, I will, if he's owt like. But if he's had a drop he can turn a bit funny tha knows."

She didn't stop to think what he was going on about. She was just thankful that she needn't go into the bar.

Ted disappeared through the doors and in a few seconds Rob came outside. He stood for a few minutes looking around, for Ada had hidden in Jackson's shop doorway. She called out to him, noticing as he came near her that his eyes were red and glassy.

"What is it then, Ada? I was just in the middle of a game. What do you want? It had better be important." He spoke sharply and Ada's temper flared. As if she would lower herself to do owt like this unless it was important.

"It's bloody important all right — I'm expecting," she snapped and in her anger speaking louder than she meant to.

Rob looked stunned and then quickly composed himself. "Are you sure?" His tone was more gentle.

"Of course I'm sure. Do you reckon I'd come here like this for owt else?" she snapped again.

"Keep your voice down then. We don't want everybody to know."

"Well, they soon will know won't they? Ada Tanner's been having a bit of how's your father. That'll give 'em all a laugh." She spoke bitterly and looked up at him.

"Not hanky panky, Ada — we didn't have hanky panky — it was more than that and you know it."

"Aye, well, what are we going to do about it? I've thought about getting rid. Old Maisy Walters up Back Street would do it for a fiver."

His reaction startled her. With a sweep of his right hand, and without saying a word, he smacked her hard across the face — a full blow that sent her reeling. Ada was terrified. No-one had ever treated her like this before — no-one would have dared.

"I'm not having no bairn of mine got rid of by some old back street witch sticking a needle into it. Get that straight."

She had no answer and stood holding her face and glaring up at him. "That was no reason to clout me," she cried, almost in tears.

"It was, if you're going to act like that."

He moved towards her and she was thinking he was going to hit her again so she backed away. But instead, he gently placed his arm around her shoulders.

"Don't worry, we'll work something out."

"The only way we could work this lot out is for you to wed me." She tried to keep the desperation out of her voice.

He paused before finally saying, "Then that's what we'll do — we'll get wed." And then he smiled — really smiled for the first time since she had met him.

"You know, it's quite a feather in our caps. Two old 'uns like us having a bairn," he laughed.

64

"You mean you want to marry me? And you want the bairn? Are you sure?"

"Yes, I'm sure. You're a good woman, Ada. The best I've ever known and I reckon if we try we'll make a right go of things."

"What about Dad and our Aggie?" she asked, panic taking over again.

"Oh, bugger them — well Aggie anyway. I'll come and see the old man tomorrow night. We'll tell him together. But bugger the rest. It's nowt to do with them. Get off home now. I'll see you tomorrow night about six. I'll come down to your place." He kissed her and without more ado went back into the pub.

She leaned up the doorway, feeling dizzy from all the uncertainty. Her mind was whirling round and round. Married again — and a bairn — by hek, life wasn't half funny and hers was funnier than most. But Rob seemed certain of what he wanted and she was more than willing to go along with him.

"Come on lass, best get home to bed. Tomorrow will be a long hard day," she murmured to herself and turned out of the doorway.

She felt rather than heard someone in the next doorway, the new bicycle shop, and turning, saw Aggie stood there, her face distorted in hate and jealousy.

"Mucky bitch. You've brought your eggs to a fine market." Her voice was rasping and gutteral, full of anger.

"What the hell are you doing here? How long have you been listening?"

"I've heard it all, you filthy whore. You're nowt but a street walker. You want putting in with a field of stallions."

Ada gasped at the depth of Aggie's venom. Was this a taste of things to come?

CHAPTER TEN

Aggie's bitterness had stunned Ada for a moment, then, as always, her fighting spirit rose. She thought of Dad. He wasn't going to learn about this mess from Aggie.

"You shut your gob or I'll shut it for you. And if you say owt to our Dad, Aggie, afore we tell him, I'll bloody murder you, I'll swing for you." She hissed the words through clenched teeth, and then in a softer tone added, "Do what you like to me, but just think on our Dad. He's getting on now and I don't want him hurt more than he needs. Things are bad enough as it is."

"You should have thought about that before you lifted your skirts for blokes — first Billy Acton and now yon one. By hell, Ada Tanner, it's a damn good job our Mam and old Polly's gone. And what about Gertie? What will she have to say about her fine sister-in-law? Have you thought about that?"

Ada hadn't. In fact throughout the whole sorry affair she'd not given a thought to anyone else at all and now she alone would have to carry the consequences.

"I don't lift my skirts for anybody, you know that, and anyroad if you'd had your way you'd give your eye teeth to be in my place now. You're just jealous, our Aggie, sheer bloody jealous."

They walked down the street and as Ada finished speaking Aggie moved her shoulder, deliberately, and giving a shove sent Ada sprawling into the gutter. She laughed jeeringly.

"That's just where you belong Ada — in the gutter," she sneered.

Ada was dazed and looked up at her sister through a blur. Who would have thought owt like this could happen in only a few months. Only a few months ago they were as close as sisters could be and now — well, they say hell hath no fury like a woman scorned.

"If you hurt me or harm this baby I'll have you for assault," she shouted after Aggie's swiftly retreating figure.

Gingerly she got up, brushed herself down, and walked as steadily as she could towards home. She wondered just what kind of a mess she had really got herself into. There was no doubt that she was greatly attracted to Rob. But love, well, whether she really loved him took some thinking about. In the back of her mind there hung a nagging doubt, something that she just could not put her finger on. Maybe it was because he was so different to Wilf. Wilf! What would he think to all this? Oh why did he have to die, why couldn't he have come home and the bairn she was carrying be his? She walked aimlessly, thinking of the excitement if she and Wilf had been having a bairn. Oh, he would have been over the moon. Quietly she let herself in the house and without even taking her clothes off lay upon the bed to sleep restlessly.

She woke just before six and hearing someone downstairs went to see if her Dad was up and getting a cup of tea. She crept down the stairs and almost fell over the straw suitcase at the corner of the banister. She paid it no heed thinking it was some hand washing ready for delivery. As she entered the kitchen, Aggie confronted her.

"I want me money." The words fell into hostile air and Ada looked at her sister, who stood by the table with her hat and coat on.

"Money, what money, and what the hell for?" Ada asked.

"I'm going. I'm not stopping under the same roof as you, not with all this carry on. I know you put up money for the laundry, but I've worked damn hard and I want my dues."

"If I gave you what you really deserve you'd get a surprise," Ada thought, but only said, "Where do you reckon you're going then?"

"Oh, I've got a place, don't you fret — and it's decent."

"It's too early for riddles, Aggie. If you want to go then bloody well go. Leave me in a mess with the work, and our Dad, as well as the state I'm in. Don't show me any mercy. Clear off and I'll get what you're due when the bank opens. You can call for it later this afternoon."

By now Ada was desperately in need of a drink. That was all she could think of — sitting down with a strong cup of tea. Maybe it would be for the best if Aggie did go. Things had got so bad that one of them had to go. No home could house such bitter feelings.

"I know you keep money in the house. I'm not coming back here once I've left. Give me what you have and it'll do."

Oh aye, trust Aggie to know about things like that. Wearily she trudged upstairs and got the tin box that held the takings. She counted out over a hundred pounds and took it down.

"There's a hundred quid or more here. Will that do? Don't forget my lass, once you've taken it, that's the end."

Aggie just grabbed the folded notes and stalked out of the kitchen.

Ada's sigh was one of relief as she heard the bang of the front door. Thom called down, wondering where his morning cup of tea had got to. She busied herself measuring the tea into the pot and then brewing up the dark brown liquid. All the time she was wondering what to tell her Dad, how to tell him. It was going to be the hardest job she'd ever had to do.

When she took up his mug of tea she found him sat up in bed smiling as she entered the room. She stood by the bedside as he sipped, not knowing what to do next.

"What was all that row about then — you and Aggie having another go?" He looked at her over the rim of his mug.

"She's gone Dad, left home, God know's where, but she's off. Been planning this for a bit if you ask me." The words poured out.

"Owt to do with that chap of yours and the fact that you're expecting?" He said the words slowly, never once taking his eyes off her face.

Ada was utterly taken aback. First by Thom being such a wily old bird and second by the gentleness of his tone.

"How did you know, Dad? You old devil, I've been messing myself wondering how to tell you. But you're right. I'm expecting and at my age. I expect you want me to go and all. Once I've gone our Aggie will come back and see to you. I'll find somewhere by the end of the week."

Tears were pouring down her cheeks and onto her dress. Wearily she wiped them away and then the realisation of leaving home and all she loved swept through her and she almost fell and had to grasp the chair back to compose herself.

"Now you hold hard a mite. I don't know that I fancy our Aggie all that much. That lass is all right, but she's too miserable and crabby for me. Allust puts me in mind of Sarah Ellen — your Granny Raines. What I want to know is does the bloke intend to marry you?"

"He says so, Dad. I even offered to get rid of the bairn and he went mad. Says he's coming to see you tonight, that's if you'll let him in."

"Well, he sounds as if he has got a bit of sense at least. I would have never forgiven you either if you'd got rid. Yes, he can come lass and then we'll see, eh?"

Ada could take no more. She rushed out of the bedroom and down to the kitchen where she rested her hands on the table and sobbed — sobbed as she never had done since Wilf was killed.

Once the flood was over she calmed down and the day passed

68

slowly but uneventfully. Molly — good old Molly — never asked where Aggie was. Nobody did. Maybe it was the look on Ada's face, or maybe they were as fed up of the tensions as she was, but no-one said a word.

On the dot of six Rob knocked on the door and on answering it she was surprised to see that he had come straight from work and was still dressed in his working overalls. He might have got himself dressed up a bit . What would Dad think? She twitched her nose as they walked up the passage.

"What's that smell?" she asked.

"I've been shoeing. That's why I'm not changed. I stayed on to see to some circus horses. Does it bother you?"

"No, it's quite pleasant, once you get used to it."

She saw him brace himself as they went into the front room to face Thom. He was sitting like a ramrod in the grey horsehair armchair. Why the devil he'd insisted upon meeting in the front room she'd never know. He had put on his best navy suit and sat as if in judgement.

He looked at Rob and without waiting for any preliminaries said, "Now then. Are you going to do the right thing by my lass?"

Straight to the point, but his words made Ada almost giggle — lass, at her age!

Equally as straight Rob answered, firmly, "Yes Sir, if that's all right by you. I'm sorry for the trouble we've caused. It wasn't intended, but these things do happen you know."

Thom thought well of him for that. No daft excuses or talk of sloppy feelings or emotions. Perhaps, after all, that talk Aggie kept passing on about him wasn't all true.

For a minute the trio stood as if stuffed, awkwardly gazing at each other and then the wallpaper. Finally Thom got up. "I think we'd best go into the kitchen. I'll not ask you to sit down in these chairs with overalls on. Esther would never forgive me."

Rob looked a little puzzled and Ada smiled at the reference to Mam. As far as Thom was concerned, it was still Esther's house.

They went into the warmth of the kitchen and soon the two men were chatting away. Rob had a way with children and old folk.

"Where do you reckon on living then?" Thom asked.

"I don't know about that yet. But we'll find somewhere don't you fret."

"What's wrong with this place? I need the company and seeing as

69

me and our Ada's always got on well, I think we might as well, given a chance," Thom smiled.

And so it was arranged. After the wedding Rob and Ada would live with Thom in the old house.

But there was more to think about than just the wedding. When Ada went to see the girls the next morning she began to think about the laundry. This was a successful business, but what would it be like trying to run it as a married woman — and a mother? That would be a great responsibility because in the summer months she needed to work all the hours God sent. If Aggie had been there it would have been different. Ada on her own would not be able to manage. She decided to go and see Mrs. Price and offer the whole thing to her as a going concern. The girls could still be kept on and at the same premises. In fact it would widen the whole range of the Steam Laundry. But first she must tell the girls. She hated doing this to Lily and Molly, but it had to be done.

She called them together and told them how things stood, making no bones of the fact that she was expecting. She'd known them far too long to try and fool them, and anyway she respected them far too much. They were not happy about her giving it over, but grateful that she was seeing to it they would not be thrown out of work.

Molly hovered around after the meeting. "You know what you're doing don't you, Ada, marrying yon one, I mean?"

"Yes, I'm sure, Molly, at least as sure as I can be."

"You don't have to get wed, lass. You could keep bairn, same as I did, and I'll give you a hand."

"You've known all along, haven't you, Molly?"

"Aye, ever since you started messing about. There's something about a woman when she's being loved, loved like that I mean. You didn't change, not to us anyroad, but you became a woman again, if you see what I mean, and it showed, to me anyway."

She decided to tell Molly everything — about Rob, the bairn, the wedding and Aggie.

"I don't know where the hell she is, Molly, and I can't say as I care. It's a devil when your own desert you, but there it is. That's it," she sighed.

"I know where she is. She's up at thy Gracie's. I saw her in back yard this morning."

So that was it — Gracie's — they'd never really got on and Gracie

70

wouldn't understand with not having a family. Well she'd got one now with Aggie acting like a soft kid.

But thinking about Gracie reminded Ada that the family would soon be finding out. Isabella — what would she say — and Gertie too. Oh, it wasn't over yet, not by a long chalk.

CHAPTER ELEVEN

She felt the tension as soon as she walked into the scullery and her feelings proved to be right for as she entered the kitchen she found a small family gathering waiting for her.

Thom sat in his chair, ramming tobacco down so hard into his pipe she thought he would send the bottom through. His face was all folded in worried frowns. Her instinct was to go and put her arms around him, but this was not the moment. This looked like the moment of truth. Well, she would face it.

It was a few seconds before the tableau of Bert, Sarah and Lizzie made any attempt to speak. They just stood looking at her as if she was a piece of bad meat. Ada decided to take the bull by the horns.

"Onny three of you, then? Didn't you think to fetch our Isabella down? You could have made up a four then and had one of her bridge parties." She didn't really mean to say that, and least of all about Isabella, who didn't, by the look of things, know anything about her plight.

"You can carry on as much as you like, our Ada, but this is a fine kettle of fish. I've half a mind to give you a damn good hiding." It was Bert who spoke first.

"Go on then — if you dare. You won't be the first neither. Our Aggie shoved me in the gutter the other night. Go on, all of you, have a go at me. Give us a kick while I'm down, make you feel big and strong." Her scathing voice stilled them and then Thom spoke up.

"Ada's chap has been down to see me and I've offered them a home here. If you reckon it's owt to do with you, then say so now and let's be having it."

Sarah's bosom heaved in a laboured sigh. "That's all very well, Dad, but what happens when you go. We've as much right to stuff as they have, more really, we're the eldest."

"Oh, so that's it. Worried about inheritance are you? Well, you can have the bloody lot. Take it now if you want. Start here with this." Ada's voice rose as her anger increased and before she could stop herself she picked up her Mam's treasured china plant pot and hurled it across the room. As one man they ducked to avoid the shattering pieces.

Thom jumped up and went across to Ada. "Stop that, my lass. That won't get us anywhere. But I must say the buggers deserve it.

What would your Mam say, what would she say to all of us turning against one another? Aye, have any of you thought of that?"

She was sorry now for she could see that her Dad was upset and near to tears. He was too old for this sort of lark. Maybe it would be best if she and Rob moved out altogether.

"She's going barmy if you ask me," Lizzie said. "She wants putting away afore she does any real harm."

"Wouldn't you be if you'd gone through what our Ada has? All right, this lot might be her own fault, but Wilf's job wasn't nor Billy Acton. And besides, haven't you ever done owt wrong, none of you?" Thom was trembling with anger and Bert stepped forward to take his arm.

"Come on Dad, this shouldn't be happening at your age. You ought to be enjoying life, not having all this bother with her. Look, I'll tell you what, you come home with me for a few days until we work this lot out. You could have a room if you wanted. Bring all this stuff and stop with us. Tilly wouldn't mind."

"That's just what you want isn't it — to get your hands on the stuff. Well, you're not. You can bloody well wait until I've gone and then if I've owt left, and if I've owt to do with it you'll not get a ha'penny, none of you. This is my home remember. I'm not that far gone that I've lost all control. I've told Ada she can stop here and that's final and I'll tell you this while I'm at it — I'm not leaving here until you carry me out in a wooden overcoat."

Bert tried again to get Thom to sit down and it so angered the old man that he raised his stick and banged it down on the white-topped table so hard it broke in two.

Bert jumped back and this time Ada couldn't stop laughing.

"You daft devils, go home and calm down a bit, and then come back and listen to my side of the story. Oh you've no need to tell me. I can see our Aggie's had her innings in. Come back when me and Dad have company — even numbers up a bit."

"You're a bad 'un, our Ada. This is all your doing. Just think on what would Wilf think to it all. Aye, have you thought on that?"

In a cold calm voice she answered, "Wilf's dead, I'm alive, but yes you're right. He might be ashamed of me. But there's things in us all that come to the top at times. Maybe this is my time."

"We haven't finished Ada, not by a long chalk. You'll hear more , maybe from a higher authority an' all," Bert said.

"I'm sure I shall, and mostly about money and like no doubt," she snorted and followed them to the door to give vent to her feelings by banging it so hard the echo rang down the street.

Dinner was forgotten and so she made a cup of tea and then faced Thom.

"I'm going up to the laundry this afternoon, Dad. I've decided to sell out and just keep house and look after bairn."

Thom looked at her silently. "You know, lass, I've never somehow thought of you as a wife and mother. I allust pictured you and Wilf in that business you planned, never thought about bairns or owt like that."

She sighed. Dad was right. It didn't somehow fit her character. Well, now it would ruddy well have to.

Mrs. Price grabbed the offer of Ada's little domain and without any hesitation offered far more than she expected. With that little lot added to the bank account she would be well set up, no matter what happened. It gave a feeling of security — no warmth, but at least they would manage for brass.

"Who is your solicitor so that we can get the formalities over as soon as possible?" Mrs. Price asked.

Ada flinched. Solicitors, well it would be Ralph again. What would he have to say to all this?

She told Mrs. Price and said that she would go down straight away. The thought of facing Ralph became more daunting with every step. Well, what was it to do with him anyway? She didn't have to give her reasons for selling did she, that was her business. But she was glad she had dressed smartly in her suit and that no-one could tell — yet — of her condition.

"Ada, how grand to see you again. It's been far too long since we met. How are you?" Ralph greeted her as warmly as ever.

Briefly she told him her business and saw his eyebrows rise in surprise.

"Is this an offer you can't refuse, or is there some other reason for you giving up what looks to me like a thriving business?" he asked.

"Yes — well — no — well — the truth is I'm getting wed again."

She saw his colour rise and the disappointment cover his face. "Might I ask who the lucky fellow is?"

And again, without any frills, she told him about Rob.

"He's got a good trade. We shall be all right."

"You don't sound too sure, Ada. Are you sure you're telling me the whole truth? There's no other trouble is there? I'd like to help,

74

you know. Of course you know. I've always felt deeply for you."

"You've not wed then?" she asked.

Slowly he shook his head. "No-one has attracted me in the way that you have, Ada. Come on, what is at the bottom of all this?" His choice of words made her laugh.

"Bottom — bottom — that's just it — it's my bottom that's the trouble. I should have sat on it. Instead I've gone and got myself into trouble — I'm expecting a bairn." The words tumbled out amid tears, sobs and sighs.

Ralph gave her a deep look.

"Oh, don't look at me like that. I didn't mean it to happen. You've no idea what I've been through since I lost Wilf. If he hadn't been killed none of this lot would have happened."

The sobs rose until they frightened him and he got up and put his arms around her.

"Ada — Ada — I didn't mean anything. Look, do you love this man — really? Couldn't we work something out. Why not marry me? He's a complete stranger to you. You know me, I would look after you. Oh Ada, I would dearly love to take care of you."

"And the bairn? What about the bairn? Would you dearly love to look after that and all?"

"Yes, if it meant that I could have you at my side. Yes I would bring it up as if it was my own."

"And the talk — could you take that? Don't be daft, lad. A scandal like this would ruin you. Oh, I'm sorry I went on so, but it's been a relief. No, best leave things as they are. But thanks all the same."

She got up and standing on tip toe reached his mouth and gave him a sweet brief kiss upon the lips. He made no attempt to hold the kiss, but he enclosed her in his arms and for a few precious moments held her tenderly against his shoulder.

"Ada, I want you to remember what I say. If ever, at any time, you need me, come. I shall be here. Promise me Ada, promise me you will turn to me."

"Yes, I'll do that, don't you worry. But please God I shan't need you — only as a friend and maybe that's not such a good idea either."

"What do Isabella and George say to all this?"

With a start, she realised that as far as she knew, Isabella had no idea.

"Tell her Ada, tell her yourself and do it as soon as possible."

She nodded and then left the office. Well, there was no time like the present. She'd go up to Sewerby and face Isabella now. She walked the oh so familiar path. Memories flooded through her heart and mind: memories of a shy, blonde little lad and then the man he grew to be. By the time she got to the hall tears were rolling down her cheeks. She pressed on the bell and was relieved to find Isabella opening the door.

"I saw you coming up the drive. Come on, love, I've been waiting for you."

Ada fell into her sister's arms and sobbed. Today had all been too much and her condition didn't help matters.

"You knew then?" she asked.

Isabella nodded. "Of course. You didn't think they'd not tell me, did you?" she laughed.

"You aren't mad?" Ada asked in surprise.

"I'm disappointed, Ada. But mad — no — remember I once stood where you are now. I know what it's like."

And Ada remembered. Of course, Isabella and George had to get wed. Their eyes met and like school girls they started to giggle.

"You daft bugger — at your age — you're old enough to know better," Isabella laughed. "Anyway, when are we going to meet this bloke that's turned your world upside down? You'd better get him up here."

It was a sobering thought. Rob up here. Somehow she didn't think he would fit in at all. Rob was different — an unknown entity.

CHAPTER TWELVE

With a vague promise to take Rob up to the hall, Ada took her leave.

Isabella could sense that she was reluctant to show off this man who had in such a short time completely altered the course of her sister's life. She decided not to belabour the point. Ada would have to do what she thought best, but as she stood at the door and waved to the small figure as it disappeared down the drive, she felt sad, as if she was waving a final goodbye. She knew, somehow, that things would never be the same again.

With grim determination Ada put everything out of her mind and concentrated upon the wedding. Arrangements were made for it to take place at the Promenade Chapel. Saturday was chosen as the day and eleven in the morning as the time — before Rob could get to the pub. She wasn't all that sure he would turn up sober — if at all.

That was the thing about him. She was never ever sure of him — not his feelings nor his actions. Rob Clamp was a man unto himself. Not a bit like Wilf and maybe, she thought, that was a good thing. That way there could be no comparisons. Not that Rob would ever take any notice of them. Maybe it was in this uncertainty that she found his attraction, for there was no doubt at all that he attracted her. Love — well, what was love when all was said and done? But he thrilled her and made her feel a woman. That was enough to be going on with.

She asked Molly and Lily to stand for her and Rob's two sons, Cyril and Fred, came to stand for their father. It was a brief ceremony. She wore a plain brown suit and hat with a buttonhole of one red rose for decoration.

As they walked from the chapel she remarked to Molly that it was more like a ruddy funeral than a wedding party. "I wish to God somebody would smile," she said in such a strong voice that they all laughed out loud.

Thom did not attend, due to his age more than anything, but Ada knew that in his heart he didn't really want to go.

"I can't help it, love, but I keep thinking on Esther and your Wilf. I'm wondering what they're thinking to all this. And I'm wondering if you're doing the right thing by getting wed again. We could see to the bairn between us, lass. I'm not calling the bloke, but I just want you to be sure."

"I know, Dad. But we've got to think about after you're gone — and not for I want that either. But I'll be on my own then and maybe I wouldn't be able to manage. It's best this way, you'll see." She gave him a swift kiss as she went out and managed a weak smile.

A small reception was held at the Oberon Cafe, but there was no wedding cake or toasting drink, just a ham breakfast and a pot of tea.

"I like your suit, Ada, it's lovely. But I'm a bit surprised about colour," Molly said.

Ada looked down at herself. "What's up with it?" she asked.

Lily nudged Molly to stop her saying any more, but Ada urged them to say what they meant.

"Well they do say that if you wear brown to get wed in then you'll wade through trouble."

"That won't be owt fresh, will it? I've known nowt else but bother for the past few years," she answered.

"Aye, well, it's only talk. You'll make out lass. Your sort always do." Molly leaned forward and gave Ada a reassuring hug.

It almost made her cry, for although she would never have admitted it, she was missing her family, especially Isabella. Oh she would have come all right, but Ada had made up her mind not to involve her sister in any of this, and so she had not even told her when the wedding was to take place. She was even missing Aggie of all things. They might be at loggerheads now, but they had been good mates for many years. Oh hell, she thought, why did it have to happen like this? Why couldn't it have been a happy family occasion? Well, she'd done it now. For better or worse, she'd made her bed.

They left the Oberon Cafe, made their farewells and she and Rob walked home together. They walked silently up the street. He never offered to take her arm, nor indeed to look at her. He was lost deep in some thought. Maybe he was regretting it. Maybe he was thinking about someone else.

When they got home she went upstairs to change and looking in the wardrobe she realised that Rob had brought down all his things. It gave her rather a funny feeling to see his clothes hung at the side of hers.

She took the marriage certificate from her handbag and studied it closely. Ada Tanner — widow — Rob Clamp — bachelor. Mrs. Clamp. A new name, a new life. She suddenly felt queer. It was as if

78

her stomach had turned inside out. Almost in a faint she lay down on the bed.

After a few minutes Rob came upstairs to see where she had got to. When he found her lying down and she told him what had happened he smiled and patiently explained that it was fluttering — the first movement of their child.

"Good God, you know more about the job than I do. I can see I've got a lot to learn."

But having Rob to rely on made a great deal of difference. She had no Mam or sisters to tell her what was going on. To tell the truth, during the past few weeks she had not given much thought to the bairn. Arranging a wedding, getting rid of the business, and coming to terms with the man in her life had driven everything else out of her mind. But now she had felt the child it had become real — a life within her — something that was hers. It gave her a warm glow inside.

Rob lay down by her side and stroked her body. "There'll be lots of things happening now. You'll have to see the doctor again this week. We don't want owt to go wrong do we?" he said.

"No we don't, lad. Not after what we've been through we don't," she laughed bitterly.

"But you don't really mind, do you Ada? Not now we are together and have a little one to look forward to?"

She pursed her lips and then smiled at him, this man who was now her husband. "No, I don't mind lad. We've got to make best of things."

He frowned. "Making the best of things is not what I want for you, Ada. Do you know, I'll tell you something now, being married to you and having a bairn is one of the best things that ever happened to me. I've done a lot of things in my time and not many I could boast about, but today I reckon I've done one of the best things in my life."

He spoke intensely, and as the words came out his Suffolk dialect grew stronger. With a start she realised that Rob meant what he said. He was speaking from his heart. He really loved her.

"Thanks for that, love," she whispered. "I feel good about it, too. Oh, I know I go on a bit most times. It's to hide my feelings. I've been hurt before and I'm a bit loath to show what I really feel." He held her close and began to stroke her body.

They were on the point of making love when a voice called up the

79

stairs, "Are you ever coming down you two, or are you going to stop up there all day? I could murder a cup of tea." It was Thom banging his walking stick on the banister with enough force to waken the dead.

Ada and Rob laughed and rolled over. "The old bugger," she said fondly. "I reckon we'll have a right time together us three."

But Ada did not take after her mother in the duties of housework and having to be a full-time wife. At first she found the tasks irksome and tedious. For most of her life she had lived with her parents and family, and she had always been her own woman, answering to no-one. Looking after Rob's every need, and what she called nursing him and Thom, was exasperating for someone of her independent nature.

The men were very good, especially Rob, who seemed to look forward to the child more than she did. The early months of pregnancy brought no maternal feelings whatsoever and the swelling of her body was just an encumbrance when she needed to sweep under the beds. Ada attacked the housework with gusto and efficiency. She hated doing it, but as always, if she did it, then it had to be perfect.

Thom helped all he could. Not physically, for he was now a bit too old, but morally he gave all the support which she desperately needed. The rest of the family alienated her totally. Isabella had taken the hint and kept her distance, but she often sent down little notes and a dish which was supposedly for her Dad. Ada knew damn well it was for all three of them, unless Isabella thought Thom had developed an appetite like a wrestler!

"Don't take any notice of the other lot, lass, you know what they're like. They'll come round once the bairn's here. Not even they would turn their back on a bairn," Thom said.

She often wondered how she and Wilf would have got on living together day in and day out. With Rob it was rather like sharing your bed with a lodging stranger. Being in one another's company once or twice a week meant being on your best behaviour. It was entirely different living together in such intimacy. She kept on recalling Esther's saying that you never knew the devil until you were locked indoors with him. But was this being truly married, having Thom around all the time?

Whenever her brothers visited she kept well out of the way. They could get on with it as far as she cared. "They'll want me afore I want them," she would mutter.

But the months of waiting proved to be fruitful in other ways, for she found she had a skill for knitting, sewing and crocheting and the layette that grew was fit for royalty. She would sit hour after hour at the work — dresses, matinee coats, shawls, and blankets. She made so many that Rob asked if she was expecting twins.

He became more and more considerate and as her time grew near he never went out at night. He relaxed, became more at home and easy. Out of the first passions had grown a warm companionship which brought them closer together. He was patient with Thom who also grew to rely on his son-in-law as time went on. They became a tight-knit trio.

Maybe, after all, things were going to turn out all right.

CHAPTER THIRTEEN

Only once did Thom and Rob cross swords — and that was not through a family dispute.

As he had done for many, many years, Thom had followed the local football team — Bridlington United. He no longer attended the matches, but he would collar anybody who had been to the match, or heard about it, and make them relate every move that was made.

And then the team reached the final of what could only be termed a local Derby. Thom wanted more than anything on earth to see that match — Brid versus Hull. By hek, that would be something to see.

He made up his mind that he was going and started to nag at Rob. On and on he nattered — breakfast, dinner and tea, and before he went to bed.

"I shan't live to see another 'un, tha' knows," was his final thrust, and, reluctantly, Rob gave in. He wasn't all that keen on sport, but if it was going to please the old fellow it wouldn't hurt him to give up a couple of hours. These two hours turned into a pantomime that lasted much longer.

When the great day came, Thom was up at ten, dressed in his best suit, his old football colours round his neck and sitting in his bathchair in the passage. Usually they couldn't get him in the damn thing, but today, well, today was different.

"Rob won't be home for hours yet, Dad. Come on in the kitchen and let's have a drink. He'll have to change when he does get here, and have his dinner, so there's no good waiting there like that," Ada said, praying that Rob wouldn't be late home.

Saturday was twelve o'clock leaving, but, of course, on this particular one, some horses came it at half-past eleven and Rob was offered some extra brass to get them done.

He arrived home half-an-hour late to find Thom still sat in the bathchair, but in such a rage, waving his stick about in the air and bawling and shouting at the top of his voice, "You don't want to bloody well take me. I knew it all along. It's no good us going now — match'll be over before we get there."

Rob nearly laughed, but taking it all in good part he forgot about his dinner and just got himself ready to take the old man.

It went down as a family story the way that Rob and Thom

arrived at the football ground at one o'clock for a three o'clock kick-off. They were the only two solitary figures sitting in a deserted ground.

"We were the only folk apart from groundsmen. They thought I'd gone barmy and I was frozen to death. The old lad, though, he sat there like a dog with two tails, nattering away nineteen to the dozen. I had to take him round the ground to keep myself warm. One of the blokes shouted and asked if we were in training for reserves. Eh, we must have looked a pair of buggers — me shoving and panting, and the old man shouting at the top of his voice and waving his stick around."

How he and Ada laughed as he told the tale. It was the first time she had found a sense of humour in him. Trust her Dad to find it.

"Who won then?" she asked Thom.

He looked a bit puzzled before he answered. "Oh, I don't remember things like that. I reckon we did, but it was a hell of a match, wasn't it, Rob?"

"I don't reckon you ever looked at the match. You were too busy shouting to take any notice," Rob laughed, as he warmed his blue hands in front of the fire.

Thom sobered up as he looked into the flames. "Ada, I saw our Albert and he had the cheek to come and ask if I were warm enough. I told him to bugger off. He'd never have taken me out like Rob did. He's not a bad bloke this husband of yours."

Ada smiled and sighed contentedly, praying that the pair of them wouldn't catch their death of cold.

"Make a pot of tea, love, and I'll nip to Rimmington's and get some fish and chips."

"Now that's what I call thoughtful. You're a good lad," Thom praised, still full of excitement.

Rob wasn't used to any praise and looked a bit sheepish. "Well, I thought it would save Ada a bit. Did you get some rest then, love?" he asked.

But Ada, being Ada, had spent the time tidying and doing the cooking for the weekend.

Happily they sat round the fire eating fish and chips out of the newspaper.

"I reckon I've given myself indigestion. I'm off to lay down for a bit. I feel a bit funny like." Ada eased herself out of the chair and stretched. A ripping sensation ran through her body and she had to grasp hold of the table to steady her legs. She thought she was going to black out. The feeling quickly passed, but left behind a strange sensation.

Seeing her sway, Rob jumped to his feet and with one sweep lifted her up and carried her upstairs.

"You're having a lie down, my girl," he said, striding up the steps two at a time, holding her as if she were nothing more than a rag doll. "You are deceiving, you know. You look like death warmed up and you're as strong as a horse."

She wrapped her arms around his neck and a glow swept through her as he leapt the stairs. She felt safe — safe with this man — her husband — a name she had not used for Rob more than a dozen times since they were wed.

Gently he laid her down and pulled the covers round her neck. "Should we get the doctor or not?" she asked.

"No, I don't reckon so. Do you know what it was you felt downstairs?"

Ada had no idea, and Rob patiently explained that it was the baby kicking, really kicking.

"I aren't half green. I've no idea what's going on inside me. Still you've been through it all before so I suppose you must have picked up a few hints along the way."

Surprisingly she found herself jealous of his previous life, wishing that this was the first time for him too. "Did you want the other bairns — really want them I mean?" she asked.

"I've always loved kids and I've never had one yet that I didn't want — and I want this one more than any. We haven't got a bad life you and me. You're a good wife and I reckon the bairn will bring the finishing touch." He bent to kiss her as she drowsily closed her eyes and fell asleep.

Downstairs he busied himself with washing the cups and saucers and banking up the fire. Thom was fast asleep and there was a calm in the house that warmed his heart. His life had been rough from the day he ran away to join the army as a youngster of fourteen. He was a good soldier and proud of his regiment, but he got into many scrapes with his drinking and womanising. Never a man to ask questions he knew most of his troubles had been self-inflicted, but he always faced the punishment and then forgot about it. Please God he had now learned his lesson and would settle down to a calmer different life.

84

He shivered although the fire glowed brightly, perhaps remembering unfinished business. Shrugging his shoulders he sank between the feather cushions and rested his head on his hands as he leaned on the arms of the old leather chair. He wouldn't think about trouble. No good meeting it half-way. It might not even come at all.

He slept for an hour before he awoke to hear Thom asking him to mend the fire and where was Ada. He called to her saying he was going to make a cup of tea and then he and Thom would go to bed.

She came downstairs, rocking between the banister and the wall like a small whaling ship. He laughed and told her she looked like a galleon. Being small Ada showed her condition, and it was obviously a big child.

"I reckon you're having twins," he laughed.

"My God, I hope not. I don't know how I'm going to manage one let alone two. If it's twins I shall give one away," she answered back.

In spite of family hostility they were happy days. If the family came down at all Ada and Rob would go upstairs out of the way. Sometimes Ada felt she was too happy and she would worry. She had no idea what about, but it was an uncomfortable feeling that all was not as it seemed.

When they were alone she would try to draw Rob out about his former life. He would talk to her about the army and about the boys, but never a word about their mother or any other women in his life. She came to the conclusion that someone had caused him great unhappiness and that the hurt was still raw. She hoped she could make up for the pain he had borne.

As her time grew nearer, Ada stayed close to home. Everything was ready for the confinement down to the last piece of cotton wool. The doctor was booked and Molly promised to come down and look after things. Rob insisted that Peg Hartley come too. Although untrained, she was the local midwife and very well regarded by the doctors.

"You can't take any chances, Ada. You're no spring chicken and this is your first. I don't want anything to go wrong with either of you," he told her.

She found lying down her most comfortable position and spent a lot of time doing this once the daily work had been done.

During the spring the winds and tides were bad and one night they were so bad that neither of them could sleep. Rob went down to make a cup of tea and they sat up in bed sipping and talking softly together.

Suddenly they heard Thom shouting at the top of his voice. "Are you deaf both of you? There's somebody banging like hell on front door."

The wind must have deadened the sound, but Rob quickly jumped up and wrapping his shirt tails between his legs to hide himself he ran downstairs to open the door. He found Billy Acton and Frank Wright in great agitation.

"Give us a hand will you mate? Molly's cottage has caught fire and they need all the help they can get. Wind's playing hell with flames and they can't get it under control."

Rob ran upstairs and explained quickly to Ada, taking time only to pull his trousers over his long pants as he ran through the door.

"Bring Molly and the bairn here, Rob. She can stay with us till she gets somewhere else," she called after him. But he was already through the door, leaving it wide open in his haste.

When he reached the corner of the street the sight that met him was horrific. He'd seen many things — war and fighting — some too awful to think about. But this, this was one of the worst.

Flames leapt through the roof of the cottage, a brilliant red and orange that blazed with the high winds, lighting the sky like a devilish furnace.

Rob stopped, breathless, by a group of men. "Can't we do owt?" he asked.

"Firemen said best leave it to them now. Molly's place can't be saved. We've got to try and keep it from spreading."

"Where is Molly then? I'll take her and the bairn down to Ada."

The group looked puzzled and then Billy said, "Come to think of it, I've not seen her. She must be up the street in another cottage."

Rob passed from group to group looking for her, but no-one seemed to know where she had got to.

"Give us a hand, Billy. It's your bairn after all. Let's find her and then I can get back to Ada. She'll be worried sick."

CHAPTER FOURTEEN

They moved from group to group with Rob taking the initiative and asking after Molly. He began to think she was better off without Billy. He seemed a right idiot, acting as if he did not know what to do with all the bewilderment. Or was he just being clever? Rob did not really care. All he wanted was to find Ada's friend and then get away from this furnace.

A piercing scream brought both men to a standstill. Rob raised his head and followed the sound until his eyes rested on the terrified face of Molly's little lad.

"Oh you daft bugger, they're still in there. Didn't any of you have the sense to go in and have a look?" Rob asked wildly.

In vain they tried to explain that the fire was already well under way before they had noticed.

Words failed him. His thought now was to try and make at least an attempted rescue. He tore off his shirt and flung it towards the gushing hosepipe until it was soaking wet.

"Where the hell do you think you're going? Don't be barmy, man, you'll never get in there." Someone tried to restrain him, but it was no use. Rob was going to have a go, if only for Ada's sake.

He wrapped the soaking shirt back to front around his face and body, then he stood and faced the hosepipe until his shoes and trousers were equally wet. Again they tried to hold him back but, deceiving as ever with his build, he was too strong and rushed into the devouring smoke and flames without a thought for his own safety.

The ladder stairs had gone, burnt like matchsticks and now a crumpled heap of ashes. The latted floor, too, had almost gone, but the old wide strong beams that supported the whole cottage remained, smouldering and charred but still in one piece.

Rob grabbed the beam, too intent upon his task to feel the white hot heat burning into his flesh. He swung like an agile monkey up to what was left of the bedroom floor and cried out Molly's name. There was no answer. He saw what he thought to be a bundle of bedding and he grabbed it and shook it. The bundle rolled before him and he looked down on the charred remains of Ada's friend. He almost wept. This was no end for the lass.

"Mammy — Mammy." A weak little voice came through the flames and roused Rob.

"Hang on son, I'm coming. You keep shouting to me," he cried and crawled on his hands and knees towards the sound of the boy.

The lad was in his nightshirt, now blackened and burnt around his body. His face and neck were charred to the open flesh, but he was alive. Rob gently held the boy and nestled him as he cried out in pain. He wrapped his shirt around the little body and then, without giving himself time to think, he jumped through the gaping smouldering floor and ran through the bottom shell gasping and spluttering as he reached the air.

"Rob — Rob — what are you thinking of — what's that you've got there — where's Molly?" It was Ada's voice that greeted him. She had been unable to rest and against Thom's advice she'd dressed and gone to the scene.

Rob couldn't speak, for his smoke-filled lungs were heaving in the effort to breathe. As the clean air passed through his body he gulped, choked and coughed with each breath. All he could do was to look down at his wife and shake his head. He held out the little body that he had saved.

Ada moaned and then sobbed. "Oh, no — please God, no," she cried.

Rob moved the shirt that covered the boy and stricken they both stared in horror at the tiny now limp charred body of Molly's son.

A hush had fallen over the crowd and one of the firemen came forward and gently tried to take the boy, but Rob would not let go.

"Where's Acton? I want Acton. I've got something for him." His angry voice echoed down the street.

Billy Acton stepped forward, pushed by one of the bystanders who could see it developing into a nasty situation.

But Rob was too tired for that. He just held out his arms and said, "Here Billy — here's your bairn — the one you didn't have the guts or sense to save. None of you did for that matter. What the hell did you reckon was going on in there — a party? Call yourselves men? I've trodden in better," he shouted in anger.

P.C. Odling came forward and put his hand on Rob's shoulder. "That was a hell of a thing you did. You've got some guts, but come on, let's get you to the hospital and get them burns seen to."

Rob shrugged him aside. His main concern was for Ada, who was sobbing her heart out.

"Come on, lass, let's get on home. This lot can sort things out now. God, I hope they can face themselves over this, I know I couldn't." With a look of bitterness of his face he put his arm around Ada's shoulder and walked home.

Thom was up, but not dressed. He stood in his long nightshirt before a blazing fire, teapot at the ready.

"Oh Dad, you should be in bed. You'll be upsetting yourself," Ada cried.

"Don't you bother yoursen about me. I know what's been going on. Our Albert called and told me. I'm sorry about Molly and the bairn. He said what Rob had done and all. By hell, you showed them up lad, showed their true colours."

But Rob hardly heard a word the old man said. He didn't think he had been brave, just practical. What worried him more was the effect that Molly's death would have on Ada.

"What can I do for your hands and arms, love?" she asked.

"Get me some honey and clean white rags and I'll spread it on thick and then wrap them round the burnt bits."

Ada looked surprised, but she was now more used to his ways and old remedies. Rob flinched as the honey touched his raw flesh. Ada took one look at the bare bone of one hand and, with a groan, fell to the floor in a dead faint.

"Come on, Thom. You've got to give me a hand to get her on the settee."

Both men — one old and one badly injured — heaved and tugged at Ada's swollen body until they had pulled her across the kitchen floor and laid her upon the couch. A trail of thick black blood rushed from her legs.

"Come on, old lad, you stay here. I've got to get to the doctor. Something's wrong. Get some sheets and towels and put them underneath her," he instructed and then ran through the front door.

Thom did has Rob had bid and then stood looking down at Ada, feeling like a helpless child.

"We need midwife," he thought to himself and rushing into the passage he grabbed his hat and stick and bolted through the front door. He looked a sight, still in his long white nightshirt, check cap on his head and big boots on his feet.

"They might reckon I've gone dolally," he laughed. But what mattered most was that Ada needed help — Ada and the bairn.

He marched towards Peg Hartley's, pausing only as he passed Cissie's house. "She should be with our Ada at a time like this," he thought and then hurried on his mission. He hammered on Peg's door with his stick and after a few moments her head appeared at the bedroom window.

"What are you doing here, Thom — and in your nightshirt and all?" she asked.

"It's our Ada — she's been took bad — bleeding and collapsed — Rob's gone for the doctor, but I reckoned you should be there and all," he shouted.

"All right, old lad. You get off back and I'll be down in five minutes. Here put this round you." She threw down a bright yellow checked shawl.

Thom put it around his shoulders and turned away. He had done what he could. But had he? As he passed Cissie's house again he just could not resist banging his stick on the front door and shouting through the letter box, "Why aren't you with our Ada? It's your duty," he shouted and banged and banged until Cissie came to the door.

"What on earth are you doing here at this time, Dad, and only half dressed and all? Have they chucked you out?"

"That's just what you'd think. No they haven't. It's our Ada. She's dying, laying in a pool of blood. You should be there. You're family — leaving her there to die alone." He was nothing if not dramatic and seeing the effect the words had, he turned and marched off again, leaving his daughter stood on the doorstep with her mouth wide open.

When Rob got back he thought the whole world was in the kitchen. Lily had heard and was down filling the copper. Peg Hartley was with Ada, who was now covered with a blanket. But, most surprising of all, Cissie was pouring out a cup of tea which she handed to him.

"I thought it only right she should be here. I hope I ain't stepped out of place, Rob," Thom said.

"No, old lad. Finish that tea and then get upstairs for some rest. Doctor's on his way and then we'll get Ada up to bed and see how things are."

When the doctor arrived, he cleared the kitchen telling only Peg to remain for the examination.

"I'm afraid I shan't be needing you Mrs. Hartley, this is a hospital case; by the looks of things a caesarian and if we don't move quick we could lose both mother and child," he said as he stood up.

He spoke to Rob and calmly and quietly explained the position.

"I hope she's not been through all this for nothing, but I know you'll do your best, doctor." Rob's voice was tired, weary and sad.

"Well, I'll tell you now, there won't be any more children. For one thing Ada is too old and I am of the opinion, by the look of things, that we shall have to perfom a hysterectomy as well."

"You mean take everything away?" Rob had not quite realised how serious things were.

"'Fraid so. I'm going to get an ambulance and I suggest you come along too and get those burns dressed."

Rob went upstairs to tell Thom that Ada was being taken into hospital.

"Eh, I don't like it, Rob. I don't like hospitals. They took one of my mates in and he never came out. You'll stop with her, won't you, lad? I don't want owt to happen to our Ada."

Rob took the old man downstairs and asked Cissie to stay with him. Then he followed Ada, who was being carried on a canvas stretcher to the waiting ambulance.

Rob was surprised to see a small crowd had gathered outside the door. Pity Ada was unconscious. She'd have liked being the centre of attention.

"That's right, have a good look, all of you, and then go and tell Billy Acton that if owt happens to my family I'll be up there to see him," he shouted.

And then, half laughing at the look upon the faces, he leapt into the waiting ambulance.

CHAPTER FIFTEEN

The ambulance was so bumpy that Rob wondered if all the shaking would harm Ada or the baby. She was in a deep sleep from something the doctor had given her. Rob was not all that in favour of injections and drugs, but he had to believe at this stage that they knew what they were doing. They — it was always a word that amused him. Who were 'they'? — they had such a great power over the world — and usually buggered it up.

When they got to the hospital two nurses were ready and waiting to wheel Ada into the operating theatre. Rob walked beside her until one of the nurses held up her hand.

"You can't go any further, Mr. Clamp. This is out of bounds."

At that precise moment Ada opened her eyes and looked up at him drowsily. "Rob, see that Molly and the boy have a decent funeral. She'd not much to her name and I don't want her put in a pauper's grave."

"I'll see to things, don't you fret. Just get on with this lot. She'd not want you upset over her."

But Ada was past hearing. She had dropped back into a state of unconsciousness.

They led him to one of the cubicles and dressed his hands and arms.

"Who told you to put honey on?" the doctor asked.

"My mother. She was an old country woman. We couldn't afford doctors. Anyway, he'd have taken too long to get to our cottage. Mother always knew what to do."

"I'll say she did. That honey has prevented any further damage to your skin and also stopped poisoning. She was no fool your old mother."

Rob smiled with pride and then he felt a little ache in his heart. He'd not been home for ten years or more. And he never wrote. Come to think of it, they didn't really know where he was, nor anything about Ada and the babe. His mother loved the little ones. She would be so pleased he had finally settled down. Rob resolved to write to her once Ada was through this lot.

He thought of his mother's face, always with a smile of welcome, her patient, kindly ways, always forgiving. She called Rob her "varmint boy," the "black sheep" and yet she still loved him and would often say, "Just remember, lad, you can get a sweetheart any day, but not another Mother. Don't forget your home and family."

He sat in the waiting room for five hours, his thoughts flitting from one extreme to another. He thought of Mendlesham, his home, his village. Then he thought of his army life and the trouble he had waded through. And then he thought of Ada — Ada who was fighting for her life, and the bairn's too. He prayed that they would pull through that. For once in his life he could have a settled life. Who'd have thought that a little snip of a woman like Ada could have tamed him? "Well, it takes all sorts," he murmured to himself.

The nurses and maids kept him going with cups of tea and in the early hours of the morning suggested that he went home to try and get some sleep. Word of the rescue attempt had swept through the town and he found himself being regarded as something of a hero. Despite the advice it was clear that he had no intention of leaving the hospital and so they left him to doze on the wooden benches.

"I could do with a smoke," he said to one of the nurses as she brought yet another cup of tea.

"Hang on a minute, I've got some in my coat pocket. I'll fetch them and then you can go outside for a quickie. The fresh air will do you good."

She quickly returned with a packet of five Woodbines and a box of matches.

"You'll let me know when owt happens, won't you?" he asked, taking the pack gratefully.

The air was good to his face. He took deep breaths to clear his head of the hospital smells. The burns were starting to sting and he felt weak and muzzy. What a night. He reckoned the gaffer would be wondering where he'd got to. He hoped somebody would have the decency to let him know. He couldn't afford to lose his job.

Leaning up the weather-blackened wall of the hospital he closed his eyes and lifted his face to the sky. He'd never been a praying man, but now he prayed — prayed for Ada and the child, but mostly for Ada. In truth, he'd never been all that sure she wanted a child. Still, it was in God's hands now.

A voice from the door called his name and he turned to see the surgeon beckoning. Swiftly he stubbed out his cigarette and went over.

"What's up — is it over? — is she all right?" The words came in one breath.

"Yes, they are both fine. Mother and daughter are in fine fettle now. A bit of a rough passage, but they'll come through with a bit of careful nursing."

"A daughter, a little girl?" Rob grabbed the doctor's hand and pumped it up and down.

"Yes, a nine-and-a-half pounder, a real little beauty."

In his excitement Rob had forgotten all about his hands, but now he didn't even care about them. Ada was all right and they had a daughter. God was good after all.

"Get along inside and take a look at the baby, not at Ada, mind you. She's had a bad time and needs to sleep for an hour or two."

Rob followed him into the nursery to look down into one of the grey canvas cribs where his daughter lay. Tears came to his eyes. She was a right little beauty. He leaned forward and touched her face. The baby opened her eyes to reveal the bluest eyes he had ever seen. She looked up at him as if making a concentrated study of this man who was peering down at her.

"I'm your Daddy — there there — my dear," he whispered.

"Come on now, Clamp, get yourself off home. That's where I'm going. I've got surgery to do, but you must rest. Come back later and if all is well you can see Ada," the doctor said and offered him a lift home in his car. Rob refused. He wanted to walk, to blow the cobwebs away.

As he walked he was greeted by many people, some of whom he did not know. They seemed to think he had done something great by trying to rescue Molly and were affronted when he brushed away their words with a gruff, "It was a useless exercise."

Thom sat waiting for him and as soon as he heard the front door was rushing up the passage to meet him. "Is our Ada all right?" were his first words.

"Not half, old lad. You've got another granddaughter, Thom. A lovely blue-eyed nine-and-a-half pound little girl. It's been a bit rough but the doctor says they'll both be fine."

"Eh, that's grand, Rob. A little lass, eh? And what a size. Couldn't have done better myself. Life's rum you know, lad. They allust say that as one dies another's born. Police have been round to see you and undertaker and all."

He made a cup of tea and they'd just sat down when in walked Bertha and Letty. They didn't say much, but set about cooking breakfast for the two men, which they ate heartily and noisily.

Rob could have managed, but now his burns were really painful

94

and he was glad of the help although he knew they had come for Thom and not him. Still, he'd take what they'd give him for as long as it lasted.

"Can we go and see our Ada?" Bertha asked. "She'll need help, what with the operation and all. We'll see what we can do."

"By hell, there's nowt as funny as folk. Last week you wouldn't have cared if she'd lived or died. Now you want to help," Thom snorted.

Rob said nothing except to thank them for the meal. It paid to keep out of family quarrels if you could.

He rested for a short spell and then washed and changed as best he could. Thom stood watching, and seeing the difficulty he was having offered to shave him.

"I can, you know. I might be getting on a bit, but me hands are steady. Come on, lad, let's have a go. I can't make a worse job of it than you're doing."

And to Rob's amazement and fright he took from his drawer a cut-throat and proceeded to give him a close clean shave. The old man's hands were steady, but he was a bit on the heavy side.

"These razors are the best, you know," he chatted as he deftly lifted Rob's nose between his finger and thumb and shaved the hairs underneath and from this top lip.

Rob dared not laugh for fear of losing his nose and lip, but it was as good a shave as he'd ever had.

"I'll have to set you up," he laughed as he wiped away the foam.

The next job was to report to the police station and see what they wanted. He didn't relish this for he did not like any contact with the law. But he went, and as far as he could gave an account of the night's happenings.

"Will you attend the inquest, Mr. Clamp? Your evidence will be vital." the inspector asked.

But Rob wouldn't make any promises. That might mean more time off work and he had to go and square things with his boss first.

The smithy was busy and his nose twitched at the smell of burning hooves. The boss greeted him cheerily. He had heard all about Rob's actions and was genuinely pleased about Ada and the baby. He told Rob to take the rest of the week to see to his family and Molly's business.

"I don't rightly know what to do about that, boss. Who pays for what and what arrangements have to be made," he said.

"You go down and see the undertaker and find out the cost and if there's no money available come back and we'll see what we can do."

Well, that was a decent gesture.

The funeral was arranged to take place as soon as the formalities of the inquest were over. They told Rob that if the insurance didn't cover the cost then the rest could be claimed from the parish.

"For God's sake, don't do that. Ada'll go barmy. Leave it until I see her and I'll let you know," he told them.

But he had no idea where the money would come from. He had nothing to his name but his weekly wage. He thought Ada might have a little put by, but she would need that.

On the way home his eyes began to prickle. He felt overpoweringly tired and sleepy. Oh, he would be pleased to get to bed. It had been quite a day — two dead and a new life, a life that was his responsibility. He vowed to see to it that she would not know the hardship or heartbreak that he had seen.

Sleep came immediately his head touched the pillow and he was dead to the world for several hours. He might not have awoken then had Thom not taken him up a cup of his beloved tea. Rob gulped it down feeling the hot liquid course down his throat.

"I'll get up now and get us something to eat."

But Thom told him the girls had been down again and there was broth and a pie in the oven.

Rob felt niggled. What could they want? He knew they didn't care about him and a feeling began to niggle at the back of his mind. Could they suspect anything? No, they couldn't or they'd have said something before now.

But as he ate the food, the thought still lingered in his mind.

CHAPTER SIXTEEN

Ada greeted him sitting up in bed wearing a soft pink nightgown and a beautifully knitted white jacket.

"Where did all that stuff come from? You look like a queen laid out there."

"I made them myself. Have you seen the bairn? Isn't she lovely?" Her face was covered in smiles.

He went forward to kiss her, but she winced as he touched her, explaining that she was still very sore after the operation.

"We can't have any more, Rob, you realise that? This is it. But she'll make up for it all, and anyroad after what I've suffered I don't know as I'd want that lot again."

"I reckon it was Molly's job that brought it all on."

At the mention of Molly, Ada's face clouded over. "I've been thinking. I've got a bit put aside in the bank. I want you to bring my book down for me to sign. It's at the back of the kitchen table drawer. I'll sign and you can draw the money out. I want you to order a good oak coffin with brass handles and all that goes with it. Bury the bairn with her. She was a good lass and she'd have made a good wife for somebody if Billy Acton hadn't ruined her." She spoke bitterly.

The baby was brought in for Rob to hold and though the pressure on his arms hurt he suffered it gladly.

"What are you going to call her?"

"Well, if it had been a lad I was going to say after you and Wilf. But I'd not thought of a girl's name."

"How about Vesta after Vesta Tilley? I've always liked her," he suggested.

"No fear. It sounds like a box of matches — Vesta Clamp — poor little soul," she scoffed.

They deliberated for some time and finally came up with what was the only answer — the child must be called Molly, and they added Elizabeth for good measure. Molly Elizabeth Clamp. That sounded good — firm and strong with a bit of character.

Rob registered the birth on the way home and at the same time called and told the undertaker of Ada's wishes.

"That'll cost a fair bit," he said, but Rob assured him that Ada knew what she was doing and her wishes were to be carried out to the letter.

As he approached the house he saw Bertha's bike leaning underneath the front window. By hell, they weren't going to leave him alone long, and just when he wanted to have a look for the bank book.

The door was slightly open and they did not hear his footsteps in the passage. Something made him instinctively walk quietly and as he pushed the kitchen door open he saw both Bertha and Letty crouched over the kitchen drawer, intent on going through its contents.

"I never thought our Ada was worth this lot," Letty was saying.

"Well, if you think about it, she must be, with selling the business and there was her pension and that bit old Polly left her," Bertha said. "She was always careful with her brass. Whoever gets their hands on this lot will be all right."

"Aye, and it won't be you lot. But don't let me stop you ladies. Have a good look while you're at it."

They jumped guiltily as Rob spoke. "We were just looking for a tablecloth and came across Ada's papers."

"Like hell you were. I expect all of them fell out of the box as you opened it, did they? Hand them over and clear off." He spoke sharply.

"We'll put them back where they belong. It's Ada's business, not ours and not yours either. Leave them where they are." Letty closed the drawer with a bang.

Rob decided not to argue. Far better to let them get on with it and think he was going along with their wishes. He glared and they beat a hasty retreat, calling out that they had left a meal in the oven for himself and Thom.

"We're planning to go down and see Ada and the bairn tomorrow," they said.

Rob made nothing of it, but called Thom down for the meal. When they had eaten, Thom fell fast asleep. He was worn out with all the excitement. Rob had intended to wait until he had gone to bed before looking in the drawer, but the astonishment of Bertha and Letty had made him inquisitive and restless. Just how much was Ada worth?

He tried to calm down for a few more minutes, but found it impossible to contain his curiosty. He went across the kitchen and slowly opened the drawer. It creaked a little, just a small sound, but in the quiet of the kitchen it sounded like an elephant's footsteps. He jumped back and stopped in mid-air as if he was a burglar caught red-handed. Thom was still fast asleep.

"Oh, to hell with it," he thought. "Ada said I was to get it." And opening the drawer to its full extent he took out the box and laid it on the table.

Inside were both her marriage certificates, Esther's death certificate, insurance policies, the telegram telling of Wilf's death and, at last, pushed underneath everything else, was a blue Yorkshire Penny Bank book.

Slowly he opened it and looked down at the column of figures. The amounts started at five shillings dating from when she first started work. Steadily they increased to tens and then hundreds of pounds, that would be the laundry takings. Finally, the total figure. He gasped. Over three thousand pounds. By hell, that was some money.

He put the rest of the papers back, closed the drawer and sat down with the book resting on his knee. He'd never dreamt that she was worth all that. Hardly any money had been withdrawn. What couldn't he do with that lot — start up in his own business — settle off a pressing debt — have a hell of a booze-up. He'd be popular all right down in London with his old cronies.

Thom roused and quickly Rob pushed the book into his pocket and went to make a drink.

"What were they after, Rob, nosing about?" Thom asked.

Rob brushed it aside lightly saying they were looking for insurance policies ready to bury Thom. This made the old man laugh. Rob was a right lad at times.

Throughout the day, if he managed to get a few minutes on his own, he would take the book and look again at the figures. Why hadn't she said anything to him about it? Didn't she trust him? He knew she could handle brass, but this was real money.

Then he realised how each night when he had followed her to bed he would find her on her knees at the bedside. He had assumed she was saying her prayers. But was she? He lifted the lace vallance and then the chamber pot and looked underneath the bed. The light off the gas lamp was not good, but with some difficulty he could just make out a small tin trunk. Pulling and pushing he got it out, but it was locked.

This meant nothing to Rob and with one of Ada's long hairpins he deftly opened the lock to find it full of clean bed linen. He moved the pillow cases and sheets and found, neatly laid between each layer, bundles of five pound notes.

He counted them quickly and calculated that there must be at least another two or three hundred pounds. No wonder she'd never grumbled about having to manage on his wages. That's why she was never short. Ada had her own little store of money.

This was a great discovery and without thinking of any consequences he took out twenty of the notes and then pushed them roughly into his pocket. One hundred quid — that would do nicely. His mind was awhirl with plans. What a blessing he was off work for a week. Now he could arrange things without causing any interest in what he was doing.

The next afternoon, armed with a bunch of flowers and a silver bracelet for Molly, he went down to see his wife and daughter making excellent progress.

He showed her the birth certificate and her face whitened.

"What's up?" he asked. Ada shook her head, but Rob persisted.

"Come on, tell me. What's up? You look as if you've seen a ghost."

"Well, just look at the date — day and hour. She was born exactly to the hour — the day and the date that Wilf was killed. Now that's a bit more than coincidence if you ask me, it's uncanny."

"Aye —well — they say God moves in a mysterious way. Maybe she's come to replace something for us both." He laughed it off, but Ada felt uneasy about it for quite some time.

"Have they had the inquest yet?" Ada then asked.

He told her it was the following day.

"If I go on as I am, I shall be out by the end of the week. If you arrange the funeral for early next week I shall be able to go."

She was pleased with Rob's gifts and even managed to let him kiss her. She had turned out to be quite tough and was amazing the hospital staff with her recovery.

Rob spent over an hour chatting and nursing Molly. When the visiting bell went he turned as he left and said, "I might be a bit late tomorrow. I want to go down and get this lot dressed again."

She looked at him a bit old fashioned, but said nothing. She knew they had dressed his arms the night before, but decided not to question him.

The next morning he was up early, taking Thom his breakfast in bed. "Can you manage to dress yourself, old lad? I want to go down and get some things for Ada and then to the doctor's to let them look at my burns," he said.

Thom said he would be fine, he wasn't that far gone.

It was still quite early in the day as he made his way to the station and caught the first train to Driffield. He went to a cafe for a sandwich until he heard the town clock strike nine, and then made for the General Post Office.

Carefully he took the notes from his pocket and counted out fifty pounds and pushed it through the grill.

"I want to wire this money," he told the clerk and gave a name and address in Suffolk.

"What about the name and address of the sender?" the clerk asked.

"Not the address, just R. Clamp," Rob said.

He took the receipt and in spite of any misgivings at using Ada's money, he heaved a sigh of relief. That would keep madame quiet until he could think of something else.

The return train left in only half an hour and he intended to be on it for he did not want to be seen in Driffield. Once on the train its rhythmic rocking lulled him into a light sleep. The whole job had taken just three hours.

When he got back he would still have time to get his arms dressed. Good. Everything was going well. Every corner was being covered and he wouldn't have to lie to Ada. He wouldn't tell her anything, but he wouldn't have to lie.

When the dressing was removed they showed the flesh to be healing well.

"I'll just put a lighter bandage on to keep out the dirt, but unless they inflame I don't think I need to see you again. Don't do any rough work with them for another week to be on the safe side," he was warned.

He needed a drink and called in at the first pub. He was soon recognised and people began to buy him drinks. He remembered the money in his pocket and ordered drinks all round.

At closing time he was well and truly oiled. He ignored offers of help and stumbled through the door in a drunken stupour. The pavement swayed and rose up in waves to meet him. His hat was askew and his eyes bloodshot and watery. He made for the Town Hall gardens and laid down on the latted wooden seat.

Letty and Bertha were on their way to see Ada and decided to

101

take the short cut through the Town Hall gardens. They were chatting away when they saw the body lying on the bench.

"Somebody had a bit too much by the look of it," Letty said. She bent over the body and shouted to Bertha, who had walked away.

"Just look here — just look at this drunken sod — it's our Ada's husband. She'll go barmy when she hears about this."

"What do you expect from a bloke like him anyway?"

Their voices roused Rob, who opened his bleary eyes. Oh hell, it would be them, he thought. He tried to stand and cheekily raising his cap said, "Good afternoon ladies. No doubt your hospital conversation will be nice and spicy now we've met."

And, giving a girlish simper, he vomited at their feet.

CHAPTER SEVENTEEN

Rob gave his evidence at the inquest in a clear and decisive manner. There was no doubt whatever in his mind that if care had been taken to see that no-one was left in the fire, then Molly and her lad need not have died.

From the evidence of the Fire Officer, the conclusion was drawn that the fire had been started by a candle dropping onto the feather quilt. A verdict of accidental death was recorded.

When the coroner announced it Rob could not stop himself from shouting out to the public gallery that if they'd got going and not just been nosing around then they could have been got out before the cottage became an inferno.

The coroner, though obviously in agreement, told Rob to calm down. "We are aware that the deceased was a close friend of your wife's and we offer our sympathy — for what it is worth," he said.

Ada was now getting up in the afternoon and was told that if she continued in this way she could go home for the weekend if the stitches had been removed. She might have to spend some time in bed, but providing there was someone to help her with the baby then she would be discharged. She lost no time in organising Lily and Peg to help.

"I'm going to Molly's funeral you know, Doctor. It'll not be long and if I take care I'll be all right. I'm a strong lass tha' knows," she informed rather than asked.

"If you're that set on it, Ada, I'll arrange a bathchair for you. I know once you've made up your mind it's useless to try and change it. But use the chair or I'll not be responsible for the consequences."

No mention had been made of Rob's encounter with her sisters. He wondered if they had told her and she was leaving it until she got home or whether they had decided not to mention it until she was stronger. He couldn't see them letting it pass.

He was right, for Bertha and Letty had not lost any time in retelling the story. Ada brushed them aside saying that if they'd been through as much as Rob in the past few days they might have done exactly the same. She didn't want to know about it — the matter was closed.

On the day she was expected home, a big, navy blue Silver Cross pram arrived. Rob looked surprised when it was delivered and was told that it had been ordered and paid for months ago.

"You know our Ada, Rob. She'd have things ready," Thom told him.

Rob was realising that he wasn't the only dark horse — Ada had pulled a few surprises.

He began to wonder how he was going to cover up the missing hundred quid, and how he was going to explain where it had gone? He'd have to start thinking fast.

During the first few days, Ada tired very easily, but with the help of Lily and Peg, and some of her sisters dropping in, they managed well. She was good with her bairn, showing that motherhood came surprisingly to her. She became so engrossed that Rob wondered if there would be a place for him in her life.

He took a couple of hours off to take her to Molly's funeral and, gritting her teeth, she managed to walk without the aid of a bathchair.

It attracted the attention of crowds who gathered by the road side to look. "Not to pay respect, just to see what her box was like," Ada said through her tears. But they were also hoping for a confrontation with Ada and Billy Acton.

Rob had forestalled this by calling to tell him not to attend. If he did then he could take the consequences. "You didn't care a jot for them in life, so leave 'em alone in death. Let them that cared see them off," Rob said wisely. Billy heeded the warning.

But as is the way of the world, it was a nine-day wonder and Molly and her little son were soon forgotten.

Ada's family became quite pally and there was no doubt that they doted on the child. Never was a baby taken out for so many walks, nursed and cuddled so much, or had so many different outfits and toys. They were still distant with Rob, but Ada assured him that would soon pass. But Aggie never came nigh nor by.

He made sure not to repeat his drunken exploit but managed to get a quick drink now and again. Sometimes he would go out at night, but never stayed long. He felt at home in the house with Thom and his family: he felt at peace watching Ada with Molly, a peace that he had never before known and never dreamt would be his.

The baby grew contentedly and there were many arguments about whom she resembled. Her eyes were electric blue with an expression very like her father's. Her hair, however, was blonde, just like Thom's used to be.

104

"I don't reckon I've had owt to do with her," Ada laughed, contentedly, as life took on a pattern of safety that lulled Rob into a feeling of false security.

Every Saturday he would go home from work, have a swill down in the wooden tub in front of the fire, eat his fish and chips and settle down to a short nap before taking Ada and Molly down town to do the shopping.

One rainy Saturday he was dozing in the chair by the front window. Slowly he opened his eyes, drifting between sleep and consciousness, looking up at the raindrops pattering on the pane. Suddenly he was wide awake, his heart pounding so loudly and rapidly he thought Ada would hear it in the kitchen.

His face paled as he saw the uniformed policeman lean his cycle under the window sill. He sensed it was an official visit. He had been expecting it for a long time. Well, you had to pay for what you'd done and God knows he was never afraid of facing the music. But why — sometimes why — couldn't he be allowed a little happiness and peace?

Since he had found Ada and Molly had been born, he had known a kind of life that before had only been a dream. For the first time in his life he felt wanted — needed — a whole man. The simple acts of going to work, coming home, and playing with the child — even caring for old Thom — it had been so good, oh so good.

Ada came into the room, holding a squirming Molly on her hip. "There's P.C. Walters at the door. What's he want?" she asked, not in the least bit worried.

Rob looked her straight in the face and said softly, "Me, I reckon."

"What for, have you pinched somebody's bike?" she laughed.

The heavy knocking on the front door silenced her laughter. She felt this was something serious, something that was going to affect their whole future.

"Let him in, Ada," Rob said.

He heard the heavy tread of boots on the tiled floor and heard a voice saying to Ada, "Don't fret, lass. I'll do all I can."

"What's it all about, Rob?" she asked, fear creeping into her words.

P.C. Walters took out his notebook, carefully licked his pencil and, wearing an official look, faced Rob across the oak table.

"Robert Clamp, did you, during the last year, go through a form of marriage with one Ada Tanner whilst still married to one Kathleen Clamp?" he challenged.

"That's right," came the reply.

"Then I arrest you on a charge of bigamy and must ask you to accompany me to the station where you will be formally charged and questioned." He was then given the formal caution.

The official words meant nothing to him. The stricken look on Ada's face tore through his heart like a knife as she uttered, "Oh no — please God no."

Thom had heard voices and noises and came through to see what was going on. Briefly Ada told him, but the old man didn't seem to take it in. He leaned heavily on his stick and sighed. He was too old for this lark.

"Can I come with him?" Ada asked.

"No, lass. It's best not to. I'll see that he gets home tonight," P.C. Walters said.

Rob took his hat and jacket from the stand and together he and P.C. Walters left the house. He could not look at Ada, but as they left the house his eyes lingered up at the windows.

"Come on then, let's get it over with," he spoke sharply. And with his back straight, eyes firmly fixed ahead, he almost marched, as the soldier he once was, past the gathering crowd of inquisitive neighbours.

Like a tableau, Ada was still holding Molly and Thom was leaning on his stick. Sadness filled the old man and terror his daughter.

"We can't do owt until we know more, lass. How about a drink. By hell, our lot will have a field day on this," Thom broke the silence.

Calmly and automatically she laid Molly in her pram and made the drink. She felt nothing — numb and cold as if she had been out in the cold morning air. She coughed as she drank the hot sweet tea and then realised that Tham had put a little drop of something in it. They sat for what seemed like hours, not speaking and hardly breathing, just locked together in thought.

At six she roused herself, fed Molly and put her to bed and asked Thom if he wanted a meal.

"No thanks, love, it would choke me. Just make a drink," he said, and she made yet another of an endless stream of pots of tea.

"You get off to bed, Dad. I'm going to wait up. You don't want to knock yourself up over this. It'll maybe be nowt," she spoke gently.

"Aye, I'll do that. If they let him home, you'll not want me in the way. You'll need to talk."

She helped him out of his chair and as she stood up she realised how he had aged, how weak he was. He placed a gnarled hand on her shoulder for support and the touch broke the spell. Ada laid her head on his shoulder and sobbed.

"Dad, what am I going to do? I can't take any more, I can't," she cried.

"That you can. We don't give in that easily. You wait and see what Rob's got to say when he gets back. He's not all bad you know and, Ada, don't take on. Give the bloke a chance to say his piece."

"I hope you're right, Dad — I only hope you're right."

After settling Thom, she checked on Molly, standing for a while to look down at the blonde head on the pillow. Dad was right, he couldn't be all bad and have a bairn like this.

Downstairs she poked the fire and settled down to wait. She realised now that there had always been something about Rob, something behind him. For one thing, she was missing a hundred quid. She knew damn well he'd got it, but she'd never said anything. She didn't know why. Normally she'd have played hell. It might have been to avoid a lie — or the truth.

A light tap on the door startled her and on answering it she found Rob standing on the step.

"Couldn't you come in?" she snapped.

"Can I come in? I thought you might not want me back," he answered.

"Don't be such a silly bugger. Whatever you've done you're still Molly's father and I'm going to see that you stand by us both."

Good old Ada, he might have expected this reaction. Oh he'd pay for it all right, but it would be a labour of love if she would stand by him.

CHAPTER EIGHTEEN

"Hold on a minute, I need to swill down," he said, wanting to get the feel of the police station cell from his body. It had been clean enough but the stench of strong carbolic disinfectant hung around him like a shroud. He went into the scullery and dropping all his clothes swilled his entire body with cold water. The next thing was to face the music — Ada's music.

Slowly, he went down the passage and then stood in the door of the front room where Ada was waiting expectantly for some explanation. And what a job that would be. He didn't honestly know where to start and then decided that the only place was the very beginning — the day when at the age of thirteen he ran away from the sleepy Suffolk village to join the army, to find a new life. How he wished he had stopped at home.

Ada listened patiently. She longed to chime in, but this was too serious. Rob had to be heard out.

"Mother bought me out after the first few months, but I soon ran off again and she let me stay. I loved the army life, Ada.

"It was when I was stationed in London with the Guards that I met Sophie. She was a dancer at the Tivoli and we fell madly in love. She came from my part of the world and wanted to get away like I did. That gave us a a a strong bond. I was only twenty when we got married — we had to like, but I was glad, for it meant that she was mine."

He paused then for a long time, lost in the dreams of yesteryear. Ada thought that was it and made to get up, but with a wave of his hand he motioned her to sit down.

"We were so happy. She got more beautiful as the years went on and I took her with me wherever I was stationed. Oh, many a bloke fancied her, but my Sophie was not interested."

At the end of his term of service he decided to sign on. They were given a little house at Aldershot barracks and it was there that 'flu struck down Sophie and his baby daughter when she was only a few weeks old.

She watched as he bit his lip to hide the emotion.

"If she's dead, then what's all this about?" Ada asked.

"Well, just listen. Now you know why I'm so thrilled with Molly — how I come to be handy about the house and that — how I know so much about the theatre. I was left with three young lads and a choice of either coming out of the army to make a home for them or putting them in an orphanage.

"I was persuaded to put them in an army orphanage at first, but when I went to see them, the poor little buggers were so unhappy and lost I couldn't leave them — so I came out and brought them up myself for a few years."

Ada listened fascinated as his story unfolded. He got a job as a village blacksmith in Lincolnshire. It had a house with the job so he took a housekeeper — Kathleen — Kathleen Maloney.

"Well, you know what I'm like, it weren't long afore we were sleeping together and I tried to do the decent thing and get married. As soon as that ring got settled on her finger she changed — my God how she changed. She became the storybook stepmother and dominating wife."

He stuck it out until the lads were old enough to join the army and then slung his hook and left early one Easter Monday morning without saying a word to anybody. Kathleen was not daft and had, through his army pension, traced him to many places to get maintenance.

"It was a daft trick of sending her money from Driffield. That gave the game away. That's where your hundred quid went, Ada," he spoke sheepishly and sighed.

Ada waited again to see if he had any more to say. But no. As far as Rob was concerned he had told his story.

"What do you want to do now, then?" she asked.

"I've tried for a divorce, but she won't give it. Something to do with her religion or something."

"What happens now then? Are they taking it further?"

"Oh aye. Kathleen will see to that. She'll have her pound of flesh. I shall be tried. But it's no more than I've been expecting. What I want to know is, how do we stand?"

"Well, we've got the bairn. She's more important than owt else. None of this is going to touch her. You'll stay here and we'll see what happens."

Relief shone over his face and he went over to embrace her. Ada backed way.

"You can stop that lark, my lad. We're not wed, you know. You can stop here, but you'll sleep in spare room on your own. We'll see what happens afore we start messing about. We've done enough as it is."

He almost laughed at her reasoning. Before they were wed she had been as keen on him messing about, but now, well, circumstances had changed a bit.

Meekly he went upstairs to take all his things to the spare room. As soon as his head touched the pillow he flaked out, lost in the sleep of the bereft.

Ada felt lost as she sank in the feathers of the big double bed. She half wished she had not banned Rob, but standards had to be set. She'd broken enough rules and there was the bairn to think about.

As with all bad news, the town was alive with it the next morning. The weekly paper gave an account of Rob's charge and the date of the first hearing. It spread like wildfire.

It took an hour after the papers were delivered for the whole family to go down and play hell. They tried to persuade Ada to throw Rob out and even threatened them both and the bairn with eviction if she didn't do as they wanted.

At this point, Thom butted in. He wasn't having anybody laying down the law in his house, not as long as he had strength to do it.

"I'm still master here, tha' knows. If there's any chucking out to be done I'll do it and if you carry on like this I'll start with you lot. You'd best go, and sharpish, afore I take me stick to you all. The lass needs helps, not this carry on."

Ada was glad of her Dad's support. She knew it was telling on him and she was sorry, but she needed him so much. The family left muttering threats but with Thom's voice still ringing in their ears.

"Thanks, Dad," Ada whispered, but Thom just sighed, sat down, and closed his eyes, wishing Esther was here to sort this lot out.

Rob's boss gave him a good dressing down, but said he would keep him on. There was no doubt that he was a skilled and good worker and he knew that Thom and Ada would be glad of the money coming into the house.

"But after the trial, Clamp — well — then we'll have to see what happens."

The first hearing was brief and over in only a few minutes. Rob would not let Ada attend. It was just a preliminary hearing and he was released on bail of twenty pounds. The trial was to be in three months time.

What a time of waiting. The family never kept away. There were many bitter rows and angry scenes, but in her heart of hearts Ada could not honestly blame them. She had brought so much shame on the house since Wilf had been killed. Many of her so-called friends were hostile, but not Lily. She kept going to see Ada and helping as much as she could.

"You've trodden a bitter path, Ada lass. I'm not going to throw any more stones for your feet to tread on — but . . ." she paused and pursed her lips.

"What is it, Lily? Come on, spit it out," Ada said.

"Well, have you been to see Isabella? And what about a solicitor? What about that Ralph bloke?"

Ada had to admit that she had thought about both — Ralph in particular. Isabella — well she would come if Ada wanted her. But would that be right? George was now a bit of a handful due to his war wounds and experiences. She had to run the estate and, besides, Isabella was a titled lady now. No, Ada couldn't drag her into this lot. But Ralph, well, she'd have to think about that.

"I'll see, Lily, I'll think about it."

Lily grunted and decided to give things a helping hand as she went home.

The next morning Ada received a note from Isabella telling her that Lil had told her everything.

"I did know a little about it, Ada, but decided that if you needed me then you would let me know. I don't really know what to do to help? Money? I know you don't need that. I'll take the child if you wish, and you can come here as well. But not the man. I'll take Dad too, we've plenty of room and maybe you could help around the place."

Ada bet she could. Well, a title had given "our Bella" ideas. Still, she admired the lass. She'd had a bad start, but she'd made a good job of her life — not a mess like this.

At first she was narked at Lily, and then realised the lass was only trying to help her out of this. The thought had hardly left her head when the door knocker rang through the house.

"Oh bloody hell, see who that is, Dad. I'll be late with Rob's dinner if I get talking. If it's owt to do with this bother, tell them to clear off," she snapped.

Thom ambled to the door and she heard voices — a voice she knew. She rubbed her floury hands on her pinny and ran down the passage and then stood stock still before bursting into tears. Before her stood Ralph — Ralph with his arm on Thom's shoulder. He looked at Ada and then, guiding Thom's arm, he entered the house, closed the door quietly behind him and went to Ada's side.

"Come on, Ada. Don't take on like this. We've some sorting out to do if I'm to defend this Rob Clamp of yours. Then you've got to pull yourself together. I want to see the spirit of the old Ada. Come on, let's fight."

Thom looked completely lost — and she could have kissed Ralph, and Lily too, if she had been there. This was her doing all right.

"Well come on in, then. I'll get us some tea. Rob will be here in a minute. Do you know, I'd never have thought about having a solicitor. Oh Ralph, Ralph, I am glad to see you. You always come when I'm in trouble. What would I do without you?"

Her face puckered up again, but she stopped as she heard the door open and shut, and then the heavy tread of Rob's feet. He went into the kitchen, looked at Ada, at Ralph and then Thom.

"Don't look at me, lad. I'm lost. This boke here, well it's young Tinker. He's a solicitor, come to see about your do. A solicitor, aye. I'm blessed if I know owt any more."

But Ada knew. Ada knew that she had an ally. Maybe a reluctant one, but a good one — a damn good one.

CHAPTER NINETEEN

Ralph sat, had a cup of tea and listened patiently to Rob's story. His face never moved a muscle, his eyes stayed passive, he simply listened.

"I'll have to give the matter some consideration, of course, Mr. Clamp, but I think we have a reasonable case. However, you must realise the penalty you will have to pay. I cannot see you getting away without a sentence. The thing I must do is to make it as light as possible."

Ada looked at Rob as Ralph stood up to leave. She sighed heavily. Was she making the right decision to stay with him? Should she take her chance alone — or maybe with Ralph? But what would he want with her now? No, she'd made her bed. Now she must lie on it.

"What — what will all this cost?" she asked.

"Oh, don't worry about that, Ada. I can perhaps get Legal Aid. We've been friends for too long for money to worry us." Ralph spoke softly and kindly.

Ada pulled herself up straight. "I'll have none of that, Sir. No Legal Aid and no favours. I pay too dearly for favours. I've enough put by to pay for this case."

Now Ralph sighed. She was as stubborn and independent as ever. Lucky Clamp, in spite of the circumstances.

Rob hadn't said a word. He stood taking it all in. He liked the look of this bloke, and felt his defence would be in the best hands. But there was something about the way he was acting — a bit familiar like with Ada. Still, if she did go off the rails who could blame her now?

After several interviews down at Ralph's office and some delays, the date for the hearing was finally set. Ada was summonsed to attend and Lily offered to see to Molly.

"I'll come down to the house if you like and keep an eye on your Dad, get a meal and that."

"Thanks, Lily. At least I shan't be worrying about that."

Rob was taken into custody early that morning and just before ten Ada made her way down to the court.

"You'll be all right, Dad, with Lil. I maybe won't be long," she said to Thom.

"I shan't be all right until I see you back here. And if they want

113

a character reference for him, send for me. He's not all bad, Ada."

She smiled. Dad was loyal to the bitter end.

She walked slowly down the street. Her feet dragged as if she had lead weights in her shoes. Kathleen, Rob's wife — aye his wife — was there, and Ada was surprised to find her at least ten years older than Rob. A fine woman, but well past her prime. Maybe that's why she wanted to hang onto him.

In their usual ham-fisted way, the police sat them next to each other in the witness stand. Ada didn't give a damn. She was past caring. She looked around the court. It was the first time she'd ever been inside a place like this. She saw the press stand — the papers — they would have a field day. The public stand — none of the family was there. Well, that was a surprise. She thought they'd have taken the row up.

When they brought Rob up from the cells, tears began to prick behind her eyes. She swallowed hard. She must not break down, she must not show any emotion, stiff upper lip, she would manage.

As if he sensed her emotions, Rob looked straight across at her and smiled. She simply nodded in answer.

The prosecution said that after informing the police, a policeman had been sent to Sibsey in Lincolnshire to check on the marriage certificate of Robert and Kathleen Clamp. It was as stated. They had gone through a form of marriage. He then checked the bigamous marriage and found it to have taken place.

"Are these being produced in court?" Ralph asked. This was not the usual procedure. The policeman's evidence was normally taken as evidence.

He turned to the magistrates and addressed them. "I am going to ask the clerk not to take this down in evidence on the records unless Your Worship instructs me to do so. I am actually being asked to put on the deposition the evidence of two documents, neither of which has been produced."

The prosecuting solicitor was clearly put out. "I have conducted many other similar cases at many courts, but I have never heard this point raised before," he said pompously.

"Perhaps you have not before come across such a learned gentleman," said the Clerk, Fred Dixon, a lad Ada had gone to school with. Ada stared down at him and he gave her a slight wink. By hek, they were on her side.

Rob reserved his defence and was committed for trial at the next

114

County Court Assizes to be held at Beverley. Again he was released on bail.

Outside the court a small crowd had gathered — most of it made up of the family. She squared her shoulders and taking Rob's arm made to walk through the big double doors.

"Come out back way, lass. You can slip up lane and they'll not see you." Fred Dixon had come behind her and whispered the words in her ear.

"Bugger that Fred, I've done nowt wrong. Rob can go if he wants, but I'm going out the same way I went in — through the front door."

Fred smiled to himself. Ada hadn't really changed. She still had some spark left.

Rob took her arm and they made to walk through the crowd who began jostling to get a closer view. A narrow gangway was made. Ada squared her shoulders, lifted her head and marched forward. She looked neither to the right nor left until she reached the end and there before her stood Aggie, a smirk on her face, filled with so much hatred it was frightening. Without thinking, Ada released Rob's arm and, taking a swing with her handbag, belted Aggie so hard she went flying into the crowd.

"You've asked for that ever since you pushed me in St. John Street, our Aggie. Now we're even. Take me to court for assault if you want. I don't give a damn any more. Whatever the cost, it was worth it." She was screaming at the top of her voice. Anger, frustration, fear, all took over to give vent to her feelings.

The crowd fell silent and parted to allow her and Rob to pass. She would have hit out again had Rob not grabbed her arm and pinned it down to her side.

"Come on, girl, we're in enough trouble as it is without you making things worse." He spoke firmly, but inside he was smiling at the guts Ada had shown. Oh, if only he'd met her years ago.

The case was arranged as quicky as possible. Ralph suggested that they engage a King's Counsellor to take the case. "I will make all the arrangements, and don't worry about the cost. I know you have the money, but you may need it for other things when all this is over."

"Don't you want to defend him, then?" she asked.

"It's not that, Ada. Oh hell — you know why. First, I think to get him off lightly he needs the best we can get. Second — you know

115

how I feel — and I don't want — can't bear to see you going through all this. I want to do all I can."

"Thanks, lad," she said quietly. She looked at her bank book and decided Ralph was right. She had enough and though it might cost a bit, it was going to be worth it. They had to get him as light a sentence as possible — Molly needed a father.

After the handbag scene, the family left her alone. It was almost worse than all the aggravation. At least rowing with them kept contact. The house and her life took on an unearthly feeling — the calm before the storm. She was uneasy no matter how much she tried to occupy her time.

"Do you reckon they'll put you away, then?" she kept asking Rob, who could only tell her that they would have to wait and see.

It came as a great shock, when, in spite of all the expert people they had engaged, he was given a sentence of nine months. Ralph said it was a light one. To her it seemed a lifetime. He was to serve the sentence in Hull.

As she heard the words, "You have been found guilty and I have no other way before me than to give you the minimum sentence of nine months," she thought she was going to faint. She had to hold onto the seat in front for support. A shudder ran through her body and a familiar dampness came through her stockings. Oh please God, don't let me wet myself — not now — she cried silently.

She was allowed to see Rob in the cells. He heart sank as she heard the heavy clanging of the doors and the turning of the keys as they passed through each one. He didn't say much — really what could he say? He asked her not to visit him in prison. They would meet when he had been released and see what future they could make.

"I don't know how I am going to face it on me own, Rob. If it weren't for the bairn I'd do away with myself," she cried as she sank helplessly onto the wooden chair thoughtfully placed by the police matron.

"Stop that daft talk. You go on home and see to Molly. She's more important than anything, you said that yourself," he told her.

And he was right. The bairn must not suffer. She could not bring herself to kiss him, not even to touch him. She just turned and with a brief "Tar-ra," made towards the door.

And then something stopped her. She could not have told anybody what it was, but an overpowering feeling made her turn

116

and run back to him. She took his hand and squeezing it said, "Don't you worry, lad. We'll be all right. We'll wait for you, me and Molly."

He made no reply, just looked at her through those cold blue eyes that showed not a flicker of feeling or emotion.

Dad and Lily were waiting anxiously and both shed a few tears when she gave them the verdict. Thom was shaking. Age, and all this trouble, was taking its toll.

"Dad — Dad, I'm sorry for all the trouble I've caused. I don't know what it is. I didn't ask to be born and I wish I never had been," she cried.

"Aye — well — I couldn't choose you either, we had to have what came, so it looks as if we're stuck with each other." He tried to smile but as he looked at her the tears rose again.

But it was not until the next morning when she got up at the usual time that she fully realised how alone she was. There was only her and Molly now — and Dad of course. But now — now she hadn't a soul to turn to.

CHAPTER TWENTY

With the morning came new hope. At the very least she felt a new determination to carry on and the first task was to see Rob's boss and let him know the outcome. No doubt some well-meaning soul would have already done that, but manners, to Ada anyway, demanded a personal visit.

She wanted to thank him for giving Rob a character reference, even if it was only regarding his work, but he did add that he had known Ada's family all his life and that he was sure the man concerned must have some good in him or Ada would not have taken him on. She was sure that had helped as much as anything to shorten the sentence.

First she bathed and dressed Molly, then took Thom a cup of tea, telling him what her plans were. He didn't say anything except, "Thank you, 'unny," and gave an encouraging smile.

As she went out of the house with Molly in the big navy blue pram, she felt it would have suited the situation had it been the dead of night — maybe with the bairn wrapped in a shawl and Dad stood at the door pointing to the cold, cold world. But that was not her style and she almost managed a smile at the vision of the imagined snowy night and she and Molly being cast out.

The "gaffer," as Rob always called him, took the news calmly. It was obvious he already knew, but he thanked Ada for going down and did not say that Rob was sacked or anything, just, "Well, we'll have to see what's what when he comes out." Almost half a promise, but that was better than nothing.

With the belief that it was better to get everything over and done with at one go, she carried on down to Ralph to settle his account. She could not bring herself to face him personally. She paid the cashier like any other client and left. Now, nearly all her money was gone.

She felt bitter about the outcome of the case after being advised to engage a King's Counsellor but Rob was guilty, there was no getting away from that, and they said he was lucky not to have got five years. She must be thankful for small mercies.

The money must be budgeted and there would be ample for her and Molly to manage on, and maybe, if she was very careful, enough to tide them over the first few weeks of Rob's freedom. They would manage.

But things had to be faced. She was not married now. She was a widow again — and a widow with a bairn and not eligible for any assistance. Kathleen was entitled to that. Maybe she could regain her widow's pension. She stopped at that thought and a fleeting vision of Wilf swept over her. No, she couldn't do that to him. She'd not smear his memory like that.

Her business done, she began to think about the ordinary everyday things — the meals for that week and the housework to be done. As long as she could recall, her Mam, and later herself, had run a weekly grocery bill at what was now Bilton's but previously had been Frank Etty's. She'd call in and get a bit of ham for tea. That would please Dad, and she quite fancied it herself.

The assistant hesitated and then became flustered. She was asked to go into the office cabin to speak to the owner, who stood there looking very officious.

"I am perturbed by the circumstances — er — Mrs. Clamp." He spoke slowly, deliberating upon the 'Mrs.' "It would seem now that you have no visible means of support. I'm afraid I shall have to ask you to settle the outstanding account and thereafter for your goods to be paid upon purchase."

She glowered and went towards him. He thought at first she was going to clout him. He had heard of Ada's temper. She swallowed hard and thought better of it. Then, slowly, she took out her remaining roll of notes, deliberately extracting one and holding it to the light in case it was counterfeit. Without saying a word she handed it over to a now open-mouthed gaping Mr. Bilton. He was startled at the amount she held in her hand. He recalled her thrifty ways and previous business experience. Now he regretted his hasty action.

"Well, now — er — I'm glad to see you are not destitute. I'll get the lad to cut two good slices of ham — er compliments of the house, Mrs. Clamp." He was spluttering and simpering like a spaniel after a bitch on heat.

Ada didn't bat an eyelid, but walked with great dignity through to the shop and watched the lad slice the ham and offer it to her, on his palm, for inspection.

"That's a lovely cut, Mrs. Clamp, you'll enjoy that." Mr Bilton stood at her shoulder.

Quickly she took the ham from the lad and turned. "Not half as much as you will, mate," she said and plonked the two greasy slices full on his face. It stuck to his nose and then, slowly, slid down his face and the front of his spotless white overall.

The staff gasped and the young lad could not control his laughter. Bilton looked a sight, standing in embarrassed silence with the two pieces of ham now on his shoe fronts.

Proudly, and erect, she walked out of the shop calling out that from now on she was cancelling her order and would patronise the Co-op.

Tears were near as she walked down the street, but she felt good. Her spirit had risen and she felt a sudden surge of energy. By hek, that would teach him — or anybody else — to start on her. She'd had enough.

Once she had settled down into a routine, a heaviness fell upon the house — an empty anti-climax. Thom grew weaker and weaker, old age and the worry taking its final toll.

It became more and more difficult for her to get him up and she finally called in the doctor.

"Let him rest in bed, Ada. He's done well you know and had a good life. This is the natural course of events," he said.

Duty and conscience made her let the others knew that Dad was failing. In her heart of hearts she didn't really blame them for the way they felt about Rob. God knew, she felt bad enough herself if she dwelt on it too much. And, like an invasion with the oncoming tide, they all came down together to see Thom.

At first they were quite civil. "What'll happen to you if Dad goes?" Bert asked.

"I've not thought about it. Maybe I'll take tenancy over and stop here," she answered.

"What about all stuff? There's some nice bits and we've all got a right."

"Let's wait until it happens, shall we? No doubt you've got it all sorted out before poor old lad's gone," she answered curtly. She pushed the thought to the back of her mind. Dad wouldn't go and leave her alone.

She became desperately lonely and found life hard going on her own. The days and nights merged into each other to become long grey periods that went on into weeks — no beginning — no end — just time.

She decided to ignore Rob's request not to visit and made

120

arrangements to go at least once just to see him: to see another human being who might know how she felt.

She asked Cissie to stay with Dad and Lily to have Molly. She couldn't leave Thom alone and she didn't want Molly to see her Daddy in prison.

She wrote Rob a card telling him of her intended visit and waited for an answer — but none came. She was determined to go no matter what, and when the day arrived, still without a word, she took Molly up to Lily's and then waited until Cissie came down to Thom.

As she went for the train she felt almost lighthearted. It would be good to get out and meet a few folk. She was not so sure when she stood facing the daunting red brick walls of the prison. Her courage almost failed, but she took a deep breath and pressed the bell on the great studded iron doors and waited. It was at least five minutes before a small inset door was opened and she explained her visit. She was asked for her card.

"What card? I haven't got a card," she said. The warder shook his head.

"I did write over a week ago, but I haven't had a reply. It might have got lost in the post." She stood her ground. She'd come to see Rob and she was going to stay until she did.

"It's the rules that you should have a visiting card. Anyway, come in and I'll go to the office and see what I can do."

She stepped inside and the atmosphere of the place felt heavy. Maybe she shouldn't have come after all, but she was here now and card or no ruddy card she was going to see Rob.

Another warder came into the small reception office. "We don't seem to have a card for you, Madam, and I can't promise you a visit without one — or the prisoner's permission," he said.

"You tell him I'm here and I'm not shifting until I've seen him." She spoke firmly and the warder had to smile at the fierce expression on her face.

He left and came back with a card in his hand and a smile on his face. "Clamp is not too keen, Madam, but I delivered your message and he finally agreed."

She nodded and grunted but did not answer. They ushered her into a long narrow room. It put her in mind of a bank with its long narrow counter down the middle of the room and the one half divided by a reinforced glass panel. She sat down on a stool

121

and looked over the counter to see Rob marching in between two warders. Oh dear, he looked thinner than ever and the rough muddy coloured serge of the prison uniform hung around his frame like a sack.

He did not smile or acknowledge her as she had expected, but merely looked through cold eyes and said, "Well?"

"Don't you get like that with me, mate. You want to be glad I've come to see you," she snapped.

He relented slightly, enough for him to chat in a clipped manner about Thom and Molly.

"Here, I've had her photo taken for you. I'll give it to the warder when I leave." She held it up for him to see his daughter and saw his face soften.

"My, she's grown. I wouldn't have recognised her." He smiled at last.

"She's nearly walking now — time passes quick." She could have bitten her tongue out for that remark. Time for Rob didn't pass quick.

The visit was brief and she was glad. It was hard work and made worse because they could not touch each other — no kiss, no embrace, just a wave which she half-heartedly returned. Her heart was no lighter for the visit and now she wished she had not bothered. Maybe a walk around town and a bit of dinner would cheer her up. The thought of pleasing herself, if only for a brief spell, made her feel brighter, and she ate heartily and then bought Molly a doll to play with.

The return journey was pleasant and passed in looking at the rolling countryside. It gave her a sense of freedom again and she felt better, more able to cope with life.

As she neared the house the lighthearted feeling left her as quickly as it had come. She shrugged her shoulders as if to rid them of a foreboding. She opened the door of the house and was about to call out, "It's me, Dad," when she saw Cissie, Bert, Lizzie and Bertha waiting for her. They looked very official and businesslike — not a smile of welcome, no sign of a cup of tea.

"What's this then — a reception committee?" she asked, taking off her gloves and placing them down on the table as if challenging them to a duel.

"Sort of. We've been thinking and talking things over and decided we all ought

122

to muck in and look after Dad. One of us ought to be here all the time, what with you having the bairn to see to. We can take it in turns."

"Oh aye? But what about sleeping and living arrangements? If you lot come down where are you going to be?"

"Well," Bert hesitated, before going on, "Well, we know how independent you are and like to be private — so — we've been busy making a self-contained room for you — where you can see to yourselves like."

He looked shifty and instinctively Ada knew which room they meant — the attic. She hadn't the spirit to argue. She just turned and went up the two flights of stairs that led to the attic and pushed open the door. The light shone through the one skylight window and it streamed across the room. They'd been busy all right — a bed, Molly's cot, two chairs, table, a fireside chair, a mock wardrobe hastily made with curtains, pots and pans and a Valor oil stove for heating.

Had it not been so cruel she would have laughed. She felt just like little Orphan Annie. Footsteps on the stairs made her turn to see her brother and sisters standing at the door.

"Don't bother to knock — just walk in," she said sarcastically.

"It's quite cosy though, isn't it, Ada?" Cissie asked.

She stared at them. They really thought they had done her a favour to make her self-contained. Self-contained — this was like a prison!

"You can't honestly reckon this is cosy. It's not fit for a dog let alone a bairn. It'll do for now because I've nowt else."

If they had been expecting a row then they were disappointed and her acceptance left them nonplussed. But Ada was learning when to keep her mouth shut. She had no alternative at the moment for if they turned her out then she would be really destitute. Maybe that's what they wanted. Well, they wouldn't get it, not if it was up to her.

"You can't expect any better, our Ada. You get yourself into these messes and disgrace us all. It might be a bit better if you kept yourself to yourself a bit more and didn't go gallivanting round town. Might stop the talk and make our lives a bit easier." It was Bert this time.

"After all, we've done nowt wrong." This was Bertha's two penn'orth.

"You're very lucky then. But I hope if you ever do get into trouble

123

then you get more pity than you've shown me." She sobbed out the words and banged the door in their faces.

She felt right at the bottom of the pit. Her breath rose high in her throat and the sobs ran like rough sandpaper through her body. It might be best to do away with it all, put an end to it. But there was Molly. She'd have to stick it out for her daughter's sake — nothing must touch her.

CHAPTER TWENTY-ONE

She kept her living conditions to herself, not even telling Lily about them at first. Every morning she fetched up a bucket of water and made it last the whole day. She did the washing down in the scullery, but bit by bit the rest of the house — by silent agreement — became out of bounds. Except Dad's room. She'd never let them bar her from there.

When Lily finally found out by calling unexpectedly, she went barmy. "You're like a prisoner, Ada, a ruddy prisoner. Eh, dear me, what would Wilf say to all this? If they treated a dog or a bairn like it they'd be had up," she said.

"What can I do, Lil? I've nowhere else. Who would take us in? God only knows where it's all going to end," Ada said.

It was no good asking Lil. They were pushed enough for room as it was. Nobody could help her. It was best to let things be as they were for the time being.

She kept it from Thom, too, acting when she went in to him as though nothing was amiss. Seeing him was her bright moment of the day.

But even that came to an end one Thursday night when he fell into an unconscious coma. She heard him calling her name and, dressing quickly, went down. It was Cissie's turn to be what Ada called 'on duty' but she brushed her aside and took Thom's gnarled hand in hers.

"I'm here, Dad — it's Ada," she whispered, and felt just the slightest pressure on her hand as he died.

She could not cry because she was completely drained of all emotion. She told Lil that she felt just like an empty bucket. Without making any murmur she let Bert and young Thom take over and make all the necessary arrangements. She could not have faced any more.

All things considered, they were quite decent to her and let her walk in her rightful place with Lizzie. The church was full. Floral tributes covered the path — large ones from the family and others from business people and the political parties. Ada would not join in with anyone else and sent a simple posy from her and Molly with the inscription "To the Best Dad and Friend a lass could have."

After the funeral the house seemed awesome and empty. They had told her she could stay until other arrangements were made.

Panic rose in her throat. She must get out, out of this house that held so many bitter memories.

Without thinking she put down her cup and saucer, took Molly and walked out of the house. She had no idea where she was going, blindly walking down the street, seeing nothing and no-one.

The surging sound of the sea brought her to reality and she found herself standing on the cliff top, in the place where she had stood with Wilf just before he left for France. She felt the sea drawing her. She could not stop herself. She was walking, almost running, to the very edge of the cliff. And then a voice, a voice as clear as a bell, called out to her, "No Ada — No."

She looked round, but nobody was there. It would be best to end it all — rid the family of her troubles — let Rob make a new start.

Again the voice called, "Don't be daft, Ada." It was Wilf's voice and she looked round again. As clear as day he stood there, in his uniform, just as he had done on that day.

She let go of the pram and with arms outstretched she ran towards the figure. It disappeared into the rolling green of the moss-covered cliff.

Molly started to whimper and Ada took the pram handle between her clenched fists and rocked it hard. Everything was so clear now. She must carry on.

Ada was not a great believer in divine providence, but she was absolutely sure that Wilf had come just in time to stop her doing away with herself — and maybe Molly, too.

Slower, but with a much lighter step, she started the walk home. She passed the war memorial and, from behind, where stood the Salvation Army, she heard the songsters practising "*I will cling to the old rugged cross.*" Ada joined in, almost laughing as she sang with strength, "I will cling to the old ruddy cross." She would and all. She had a right to some life — and you never know — it might get better now.

The family offered to look after her and Molly if she would promise to give Rob up. "I'm promising nowt," she snapped.

Each night she would peep into Dad's room. It was a sort of comfort to see the familiar big bed where, in childhood, they had driven imaginary horses and dustcarts. Each day she would shed a few tears as the lonely hours stretched before her. But now, she cried alone — no words of comfort from Dad — now she cried alone.

In view of the visit she did not bother to contact Rob again and with remission for good behaviour he served only just over six months of his sentence. He had made up his mind to behave and get out as soon as he could. Prison life was too cold and cruel. But not from the warders. They were a decent bunch and he supposed prison life could not be improved upon under the current circumstances. It was the human indignities that upset most of all: three men to a cell, one bucket all night for slops, lights out at eight and roll-call at six. The stench was belly-wretching and at first he could not eat because of it. He had led a hard life, but this, this was beyond it all. If ever he had needed a lesson then prison had taught him one.

It did not work with all that way. Some of his bedfellows were old hands at the game and to them it was almost a home from home: in some cases a damn sight better than life outside. He thought about the doss houses he had slept in. A clothes line for a penny a night strung across to lean your arms on. The stench of other dossers had been bad enough, but he had got away from that every morning. Here it hung around all the time. He finally ate just enough to keep him going and consequently lost a lot of weight, but not strength. Twice weekly they were allowed into the exercise yard for half-an-hour and he used these periods to the full, doing his army training exercises.

As a bigamist he came in for a lot of ragging. They soon tired however when they saw it had little or no effect on him. He was determined to keep his temper under a tight rein and only once did he let it go by sticking up for another prisoner. He made a point of not being too friendly with any of them. One or two he would chat to on a casual basis, those in for minor offences. He kept away from the heavy boys.

He more or less joined up with Artie Robson, who was serving six months for stealing from the farmer who employed him. Artie was no criminal and prison life terrified him out of his wits — that and the thought of his wife and bairns in the workhouse. He was small and meek and the others took delight in bullying and ordering him around like a skivvy. "Fetch me this, Artie — give us your snout, Artie." The little bloke would run to obey and be tripped up for his trouble as he ran. They would laugh at him sprawled on the floor. Rob didn't care for this, but kept quiet until one particular incident.

127

Battling Moule was the main tormentor. He was a one-time fairground boxer and fancied himself. Most of his crimes were robbery with assault — the use of fists, feet and anything else that came to hand. His frame was big and muscular and his face, under a shaven head, looked as if it had been spread out like greasy margarine across the features. To some unsuspecting person he was quite a frightening sight.

As the sentences progressed they were given jobs in the mail bag shop, sewing the hard canvas bags with large needles. They worked in groups of five — two cutting out, two sewing and one folding the finished bags. Talk was not actively encouraged, but some of the warders would turn a deaf ear as long as the work went on uninterrupted.

Artie, Rob, Battling Moule, Tosh McCabe and Zac Newley were grouped together. Newley and McCabe were Moule's cronies and they took delight in riling Artie and trying to get Rob annoyed. Boredom struck Moule and he decided to have some fun at Artie's expense. Throughout the whole period he taunted the little bloke, making him fetch and carry and tripping him up as he ran round.

Rob would not join in, but when Moule demanded Artie's mug of tea, he warned him to lay off. "Get somebody your own size," he tried to chaff.

"Oh blimey, we've got a hero, have we? A bloody hero that wed two women. You're a glutton for punishment, you are, Clamp. Hand that tea over here, Artie," he muttered and leaning forward stuck the large bag needle into Artie's leg.

In fear of making more trouble for himself, Artie stifled the scream that rose to his lips and whimpering handed over his mug of tea.

Moule deliberately elbowed his hand and sent the steaming liquid pouring over Rob's legs. He was going to show this skinny bit of a bloke that he wasn't afraid of him. He certainly was not prepared for what happened.

Rob, in cold white anger, threw the mail bag from his knee and got up from the bench. Moule thought he was going to ask permission to dry himself down and started to smirk. Rob did not do as expected. Instead, he slid behind Moule and, grabbing him in a tight neck hold, held him until the man was gasping desperately for breath. He brought his other hand round and grasping Moule's ear he pushed the bag needle straight through the lobe and out again. It was over in a few seconds almost before any of the others had realised what had happened.

"Don't mess with me, Moule. Stick to somebody your own size. From now on let things be," he whispered into the bleeding ear.

Now Moule was fully aware of the pain and lay screaming and shouting for a warder. He lay writhing on the floor, blood pouring from his ear.

The warder was an old hand and used to these tactics. He strolled across, almost casually, and looked down. "Fancy a big bloke like you making such a fuss over a scratch on your ear hole," he said.

"It weren't no scratch. He pushed the bloody needle right through. He wants putting on hard for this," Moule shouted.

"And you're going to look daft in front of all your mates if this gets out. You asked for that, Moule. Now, be a good lad and get up and we'll get it seen to and forgotten — right?" The tone was persuasive and firm. Moule would do as he was told.

Artie stood transfixed. He was scared out of his wits and scared for Rob too. There could be some severe consequences for this lot. When he heard the warder talking in such a quiet way, he realised that Rob had got away with it. He turned to Rob and said in the same quiet voice. "Don't go making a habit of this, Clamp. But on the Q.T., I've been waiting for somebody to give this one his dues for a long time." Without a smile or any expression on his face he escorted the furious Moule to the washroom.

"By hek, lad, that was something. I didn't think you were as strong as that. You don't look as though you could knock skin off a rice pudding," Artie laughed as he and Rob settled down in the cell for the night.

"You want to learn to look after yourself, Artie. There won't always be somebody there to help."

Shortly after this incident Rob was released. The clanging of the doors rang like music through his ears. He looked up at the sky — grey and misty, but oh so beautiful. A patch of blue shone through and he thought of Molly's eyes. He had made up his mind not to bother Ada, but now he was out, he could not resist the temptation just to see them once more. There was still no sign of divorce: he couldn't make an honest woman of Ada so it was best to clear off and let her make a life for herself, give her a chance maybe to meet someone else.

The discharge warrant paid his fare to Bridlington and as he

129

stepped from the train memories came flooding back. He smiled as he walked through the Town Hall gardens. Eh, that was a day when he got roaring drunk. He saw the sign of the 'Swan' and felt his throat tickle. He needed a drink.

He ordered a pint with a rum chaser. He needed Dutch courage to face Ada.

The landlord smiled as he served the drinks. "Just got into town have you, sir?" he asked politely.

"You could say that. As a matter of fact, I've just been released from one of His Majesty's houses — bigamy — you might remember the case — Ada Skipton." He spoke between gulps from the glass.

"Can't bring it to mind, sir," he said, obviously not all that interested.

Well, it was old news now. Rob drank the pint down in seconds and followed it neatly with the rum.

"You look as if you needed that," a voice spoke at his elbow. It was Wally Bradshaw. "I couldn't help overhearing. You've come back to Ada then. Not afore time either."

"What do you mean?" asked Rob sharply.

"Well, things aren't that good. Did you know old Thom had died? Well, the family stepped in then and I don't hold with what they've done at all."

"What have they done?" Anger was rising in Rob's voice.

"Best get up there and see for yourself. It's not my business, but Ada doesn't come out much now, not since they put her and the bairn in that attic."

Rob ran through the doors and up the street until he stood outside the old house. Without pausing, he pushed open the door and marched in to find Lizzie standing at the kitchen table.

"What the hell do you want? " she snapped.

"I want Ada," he said in a whispering voice. "And I've come to get her."

CHAPTER TWENTY-TWO

Lizzie opened her mouth as if to start a row and then shut it tight, thinking better of it.

He took the stairs two at a time, shouting Ada's name with each step. He reached the middle landing to find Ada stood there with Molly in her arms.

She looked at him, grunted, and said, "So you've come back then, have you?"

He couldn't think of anything to say. He just stood there looking at her like a gormless idiot.

"You'd best come in then and we'll have a cup of tea."

It was as if he had just returned from a holiday. No emotion, nothing.

"He's not to go up there, our Ada, you know what we said?" Lizzie shouted from the passage.

"Oh, you've been listening have you. Well you can bugger off. Go and fetch the others and chuck us out," Ada shouted back and ignoring any other abuse she might throw at them they went up into Ada's attic home.

In spite of all his wild imaginings she had made the room quite cosy. He noticed that she had lost a bit of weight but Molly was as chubby and pretty as ever. She gurgled and laughed at him as if she knew Rob was her father.

"Got any plans then?" Ada asked as she busied herself with the kettle and teapot.

"Not really. I only came to see if you were both all right. Fancy them shoving you up here. I came to tell you to forget all about me, to make a new life for yourself and Molly, but now — well."

The unfinished sentence hung between them, and then Ada gave a bitter laugh. "I'm not likely to forget you with this bundle of mischief, am I? And anyroad, who says I want to forget you after all we've been through?"

He dropped his coat and the brown paper parcel that held all his worldly goods on the little table and took them both in his arms. "If you take me on again, I won't let you down a second time. I can't marry you yet, but I will as soon as I can — I promise you that, Ada."

"You can bet your life you will, if only for her sake," she nodded towards Molly.

"No Ada, not just for her, for you and for me. To make up for all these months of waiting. I've suffered too, you know."

"I reckon you fancy yourself, Rob Clamp. How do you know I've been waiting?" She looked cheeky and pert, a little of the old Ada poking through.

"That's better, more like the Ada I knew." He bent and kissed her.

Molly didn't really like being ignored. She had been the centre of her Mammy's attention for too long. She wriggled in Ada's arms, punched Rob on the nose and shouted "Me — me — me."

He laughed, hugging her to him. "I know it's you — you — you little beauty. Come and give Daddy a kiss."

He reached out for her, but a banging door brought them down to earth again. It was Bert. Lizzie had done what Ada suggested and fetched in reinforcements.

"Don't think you're stopping under this roof. I'll ask you to leave, peaceably. We don't want any trouble," Bert said, bracing himself pompously.

"I'll not cause any bother, but I've nowhere for Ada and the bairn. I'd appreciate it if you'd let them stop on until I make arrangements." Rob spoke civilly, not wanting to cause any trouble. He was in no position to risk having them all thrown out onto the streets.

"If we've any say she'll stop here for good. She can go back to the laundry and work and Cissie and Lizzie will see to the bairn."

"I'm going with Rob. It's best for us all if I do. Come on. I'll get me coat and dress bairn and we'll go and seek lodgings." She was firm. She was staying with Rob and there'd be no changing her mind.

"You can take the consequences then, my girl. Eh, it's a good job Mam and Dad aren't here to witness it all." Bert was on his pompous horse again.

"I'll tell you this, lad. If they had been, you wouldn't be stood here and had your foot under the table with other lot. You'd have been chucked out." She was angry with herself to find tears coursing down her cheeks and Bert had the grace to look sheepish.

Rob kept out of it all. He could see the way Ada was feeling and it wouldn't do any good making things worse.

She dressed Molly and put her in the pram and walked aimlessly up the High Street.

"Wherever shall we look — who would want us like this?" Rob asked.

"I'm off up to Lily's. She'll know somebody."

And they didn't have to go any further for Lily offered him bed and lodgings until he could get something for the family.

"You could all come and live with us, love, but there just isn't the room. Rob will have to share with our Johnny as it is," she apologised.

"Don't worry, lass. You've done more than anybody for me. Rob'll soon find us somewhere." Ada spoke with more confidence than she felt.

Ada persuaded Rob to stay and have tea and not to go back down to the house with her. It was best to keep out of the way. Once he got something then they could get away and start a new life. A new life — the words stuck in her throat. She'd give all the world for a fresh start.

Slowly she walked down the familiar street pointing out the buses and houses to Molly to stem the ache in her heart. Molly sat laughing away. Nothing had affected her anyway. She was young and, please God, would never know anything about this mess.

As she came in sight of the house she saw a big box outside the front door. No doubt they were taking a few more bits out of the house. They weren't half making hay. She manoeuvred the pram round the box to reach the door, and turned the knob only to find it was locked. She banged on the door and it must have been at least five minutes before it was opened, just a little bit, and Bert stuck his nose out.

"What do you want, then?" he asked.

"You know bloody well what I want. I want to come in and go up to my room like a good girl," she said with sarcasm.

"You're not welcome here. If you intend to associate with that sort you can keep away. Your things are all in them tea chests. We don't want whores here." The door banged in her face.

In a daze, she looked at the closed door and then at the boxes. She couldn't believe that they could do this to her — not her own family. Hadn't she had enough? But turning her out — no-one would sink that low.

Biting back her tears she tried to lug the boxes and lift them onto Molly's pram, but one fell to the ground, smashing the thin plywood, and leaving her belongings strewn across the pavement.

The local policeman stopped and asked what was going on.

"It's all I've got. They've chucked me out. Because I'm sticking by Rob, they've chucked me out," she sobbed.

"Eh, never, lass. Come on and I'll give you a hand." He spoke kindly and started to pick up the clothing and belongings. He kicked the broken chest, making it thud against the closed door.

"Leave it be, lass. I only hope the first one out breaks his neck on it."

She looked up to thank him and saw that it was the man who had arrested Rob — a lifetime ago.

"Thank you, thank you. Eh, what must you think of me?" she cried.

"I don't think in my job, lass, it doesn't pay to think, but stop your blithering and let's go and get that bloke of yours and then come up with me to Brinners. They've got a couple of rooms going spare and I'll speak for you," he said.

"Speak for a jailbird?" She couldn't help the jibe.

"Aye, he's not a bad sort that Rob Clamp. Soft and easily led, but not bad."

He led the little group up the street laughing and tickling Molly, who thought it was a great joke. She rumbled in the clothes picking up garments and holding them above her head.

"Knickers — Mammy's knickers," she cried out and to Ada's shame she held up a pair of silk knickers. The funny side struck her and for a few minutes she and P.C. Walters were completely helpless with laughter.

Lily offered him a cup of tea once the situation had been explained. He refused saying that he was off straight up to the Brinners.

"I'll be back in a few minutes so be ready."

The few minutes were spent in trying to wrap up the belongings.

"We must have looked like a rag and bone lot," Ada laughed.

"But Ada, you had more stuff than this. Where is it all?" Lily asked.

"Oh, I expect they will send it to my new address," she smirked.

"Well, if the Brinners won't take you, you will have to stop here for a day or two. We'll manage somehow."

Ada smiled across at her friend. She wanted to say thank you, but at that moment she could not find the words.

P.C. Walters was as good as his word and returned in a few

minutes with the news that the Brinners would be pleased to take them in.

"They are a good living couple and like to think these good deeds are what they were sent for. I know there's many homeless been glad they do. You behave yourself now. I've given my personal reference," he warned.

It was dark as they left Lily's and the shadows of the gas lights spread eerie shadows across the pavement.

"This is a good first day out," Ada said. "Here we are, destitute."

She was a bit nervous for though she had heard of the Brinners she did not know them at all. They were folk who kept themselves to themselves, quite elderly, and she could not recall any family. Still, it would be a roof over the heads for the time being.

They both looked up at the three-storeyed house and then at each other before knocking on the door. The door opened to reveal a man of mediunm build, wearing a hand-knitted cardigan and collarless shirt.

"We're the new lodgers," Rob said.

"Oh yes, come on in. The missus took the liberty of making you a bit of tea. She thought you might need it after your little upset." He opened the door to allow room for the pram and ushered them into the dimly lit kitchen.

The gas was turned down very low, but as soon as they went in Mrs. Brinner turned it up full to show a large, spotlessly clean room in the centre of which was a family table laid with a white cloth and pots ready for a meal.

"Come in, love. Here, let me hold the baby." Mrs. Brinner lifted Molly out of the pram.

"You shouldn't have gone to all this trouble. We've not got a lot to give you in return, but I . . ." Ada broke down in tears.

"Don't take on so, lass. We all know what a bit of trouble is," Mrs. Brinner comforted.

"A bit," Ada thought, "I'm drowning in it."

CHAPTER TWENTY-THREE

After the meal they were shown to their rooms. The main one was large and fairly comfortably furnished with easy chairs, a table and chairs and a sideboard. The bedroom — not quite so big — left plenty of room for Molly's cot. Ada had forgotten about that with all the fuss. They'd have to fetch that. And there was also a small boxroom with a sink, cold water and gas stove. They would be self-contained, and have a bit of privacy at least.

"You'll be all private up here, but we'll welcome you downstairs any time you want to pop down. I'd like to give you a hand with the little girl."

Ada couldn't believe it. After all the hurt and anger they had found a haven. Maybe this was a sign of better times.

They snuggled together between the cold but clean linen sheets and as she pushed her toes to the bottom of the bed she felt the warmth of a stone hot water bottle. Molly slept between them, cuddled happily in Rob's arms.

They soon slept, but Ada kept waking up and thinking about the Brinners, and then she remembered that they had a son, a spoilt brat who was the apple of their eyes. He left home without a word, joined the army and married what they termed an unsuitable lass. He had been killed early on in the war and the lass tried to visit and bring her baby daughter to see her grandparents. They had shunned her and in her desperation the girl had killed herself, and the child.

Poor old folk, thought Ada. How funny that she should benefit from such sadness.

Early the next morning they got up and then realised that they had no food in the cupboard. But as soon as they were about there was a tap on the door and a tray of breakfast was pushed through to them. They couldn't thank the old lady enough. She had even made porridge for Molly.

"What now?" Ada asked, eyeing Rob up and down as he shaved.

She thanked God that Molly had slept between them. At the moment she could not have borne him to touch her. Give him his due, he had not tried. But before he did, Ada wanted a wedding ring on her finger — legally.

"I'm off to see if there's still a job at the smithy," he said and suggested she went with him. "We could pick up the cot and what's left," he said.

Ada wasn't sure that she wanted to call, but they needed the cot if nothing else.

Happily they walked down the street, Rob proudly pushing the pram. There seemed to be a bit of commotion near the old house and as they neared they saw Albert trying to load Mam's piano onto a handcart.

"He'll never manage that, the daft idiot," Ada sniggered. They stopped at the other side of the street to watch him struggle.

"Didn't know you could play the piano, our Bert," she called across.

Bert ignored her, being intent upon getting out of the way before he made a complete fool of himself.

"Hang on, lad, I'll come and give you a hand."

Ada crossed the road leaving Rob standing with the pram. He wondered what she was up to, but decided not to interfere. It looked like being a laugh if nothing else.

Ada walked across to her brother, who had been joined by Cissie. They struggled and leaned the piano against the handcart, stopping for a breather before the final lift.

"Come on, get a hold of it, both of you," cried Ada and as they did so she slipped and gave the handcart a shove. It went bowling down the street with Bert and Cissie hanging on to it and the end of the piano like grim death. It proved too much, and the whole thing crashed to the ground, the notes ringing out like a tuneless last chord.

"You did that on purpose," Bert shouted.

"Never. I was only trying to help — like you helped me." Ada looked the picture of innocence and then cracked out laughing.

"God doesn't pay his debts in coins, you know," she laughed and went back to an almost hysterical Rob and Molly, who was joyfully clapping her hands shouting "Me — me — me."

The gaffer acted as if he had been expecting Rob to call and without any fuss he was offered his job back at a wage of two pounds ten shillings a week — not a bad penny.

"We'll soon get turned round, you'll see," Ada told him.

The Brinners were excellent landlords. They never interfered or tried to pry and it was quite nice living there. The only thing was that the walls were not all that sound-proof. They gave very little privacy for making love.

Rob had not pestered her, but once Molly was in her cot, Ada could not resist cuddling up to him and he, being a man, could not resist making advances. At times, things got a bit strained, but they would wait until the Brinners offered to take Molly walking on Sunday afternoons and then make love in an empty house.

Ada made full use of all her thrifty ways and was soon saving money from her weekly housekeeping. She baked bread, pastries and cakes, and had one good meal a day, sometimes doing a bit extra to give to the Brinners as a little treat.

"You're a good woman, Ada. We'll miss you if you ever leave. And now you're getting on your feet you must be thinking about it?" the old lady said as they shared a cup of tea.

"No, I haven't, not really. I don't want to move until we can get married and it doesn't look as though that's going to be for a while yet," she answered.

The old couple doted on Molly and Ada decided that when they got round to christening her they would be godparents.

Each week she gave Rob ten shillings out of his pay packet and out of this he religiously sent seven-and-sixpence down to Kathleen under the Court Maintenance order. He begrudged every penny and might not have sent it had Ada not kept a firm eye upon him. She asked for the Post Office counterfoil and kept them in a drawer. There was going to be no slip-ups this time.

Every week she went to Esther and Thom's grave to take flowers and sit quietly by their side. Once or twice she met some of the family and after a time they got around to passing the time of day. She never tried to press things further.

When Molly got to three years old, Ada began to make plans for her education. She wanted her to have all the advantages of a good schooling and not to have to give it up and go out to work as she had done. She wondered if going to the High School would have changed her life at all. Perhaps she might have married old Ralph if she had.

The first step in educating Molly was Irene's Dancing School. Here Molly would learn how to move and use her limbs. She took her along one Saturday morning and enrolled her in the class. As Ada gave details to the secretary, Molly bolted and joined in the line of chorus girls, kicking her legs in the air and tapping her feet on the ground.

"This one looks like a natural. Let her stay. She looks as though

138

she's enjoying herself." And without bothering one bit, Molly stayed until the session was over.

She proved to have such a natural talent that private lessons were suggested. It meant putting a bit extra aside, but Ada agreed willingly. Rob, too, was enjoying success. He had worked diligently and the boss showed his appreciation by raising his wages to over three pounds. They were rich.

"We might be able to think about a place of our own soon," he said.

"Not yet, lad. First, I want to save enough for Molly to go to convent." A home would come with marriage.

"Aren't you going it a bit, what with dancing lessons and now the private school? And do you reckon they'll take her as things are? They might not approve." Rob tried to warn her but she took no notice.

An appointment was made to see the Mother Superior, who proved to be very understanding. Well they would be, she thought. They were getting paid for it. When she informed them about the marriage situation, Mother Superior hummed around a bit.

"I cannot say that we approve, and taking the child might give the impression that we condone the action. The whole sordid business is well known. It may react upon the character of the school." She did not speak unkindly.

"Can I ask you a straight question, Mother?" Ada said, looking her square in the face. Mother Superior nodded assent.

"Was Mary married when she conceived her baby?"

The Mother Superior stood in stunned silence and then a twinkle shone through her eyes. "Have you any Irish in you, Ada?"

"Maybe. We're not really sure, but you haven't answered my question."

"And you know very well I cannot. We'll take your little girl and be glad to do so."

Another battle over, Ada thought to herself and there'd be more to come, but for Molly she'd win them all.

Scholastically Molly was very bright and it came as rather a surprise how well she got on with her lessons and quickly made friends with other children. Ada did notice that none ever came to call or ventured near the house, but that didn't matter — not just yet it didn't. Once they got married and a place of their own then things would be different.

139

Each year the dancing school held a pantomime and Molly was given a small part in Cinderella. She also had a solo spot in which she danced and sang a popular hit, "*I'm the Little Boy that Santa Claus Forgot.*" Dressed in a brown romper suit and a cloth cap on her head she looked the part to a tee.

As she sang, Ada thought about their lonely days together in the attic — just her and Molly when it seemed that not only Santa Claus had forgotten them but the whole world. Things were better now and Ada vowed that never again as long as she had breath in her body would things sink as low as that.

The show ran for three nights and each night Ada was in the dressing room to see that Molly was ready. On the last night she asked one of the bigger girls to see to her so that she and Rob could watch from the audience. Being Ada she could not do things by half and she booked them into the best seats.

"Going it a bit, aren't we?" Rob said as they settled down with their programme clutched together with a bag of imperial mints.

"Well, she deserves all the encouragement we can give. We'll see her better from here."

Pride shone from his eyes as he looked and listened to the whole show, especially when Molly performed with such ability. She certainly didn't take after him except for her eyes and size, but it was clear that she had inherited the spirit and character of her Mam.

Neither of them applauded her acts for they felt that would be showing off too much. Ada turned to look around and see where the prolonged clapping was coming from and gasped when she saw, sitting three rows behind her, her three sisters and their families. They almost took up the whole row. What the hell had made them turn out? They didn't usually support these dos and she couldn't believe they had come for Molly, even though she had been given a good write-up in the local paper.

As they came out of the theatre Ada overhead a remark about how good that little girl was — 'The one that sang about Santa Claus.' She bristled with pride, but nearly fainted when she heard Cissie's voice saying loud and clear, "Yes, that's little Molly. She's our niece, you know, our Ada's little lass."

Forgiveness from the almighty! Ada made as if she had not seen or heard them and taking Rob's arm walked straight past to meet Molly at the stage door.

Ada had always been firm with Molly about her manners and she was to greet people she knew properly, but never to speak to strangers. On an errand to the fish and chip shop one Saturday dinner time, she bumped into Lizzie, who greeted her with, "Hello young lady."

"I don't know you and my Mammy says I'm not to speak to strangers," Molly answered curtly and primly.

"But I'm your Aunty. It's all right to speak to me," Lizzie told her and offered a sweet in encouragement.

"Aye, and I'm Rob the blacksmith's daughter and I don't know you from Adam." And with a swift retort, she skipped off after refusing the sweet.

By hell, she was a chip off the old block right enough. Lizzie couldn't help laughing to herself as she watched the tapping heels up the street, heard the kicking at the door and a loud shout of "It's me, Mam."

She felt a surge of pride starting and then brushed it away with a muttered, "I'm going soft in my old age."

CHAPTER TWENTY-FOUR

Things had been going well for some time when Rob decided to approach Kathleen about a divorce again. He would offer a larger maintenance allowance, that might do the trick. But, in spite of the two or three letters, there was no reply.

"I've decided to take next Saturday off, Ada, and go down to see her. I might as well face her and put my case. She'll be getting on a bit now and you never know might have softened," he said hopefully.

Ada smiled in reply. Well, they could but try and for the bairn's sake it might be worth it.

The journey was tedious and boring. Rob arrived to find the house locked and bolted. It looked neglected, as if it had not been lived in for some time. He tried asking at the house next door if anything was wrong.

"She died over nine months ago, mate. She hadn't anybody close, you know, and landlord has just left the house as it was."

Rob listened incredulously. He got the owner's address and went to see him, showing as proof of his identity the marriage certificate which he had brought down amongst the papers.

"There's a lot of letters waiting. Do you want to have a look? I didn't know what to do with them," he said. He handed Rob a pile, most of which were the weekly payments he had been sending.

"I'll take these. They're mine anyway. But you can do what you like with the rest of the stuff. I don't want any of it."

He was free — free — and with a bit of brass in his pocket, for the orders amounted to quite a sum.

Good old Ada for keeping up the payments and for keeping all the counterfoils. Some might be out of date, but they'd pay up once they knew the reason. It would be enough for a decent wedding and a bit of a holiday too.

He decided to tease Ada a bit, have a bit of a lark, but when he saw her he was so excited that he burst into the story straight away. Then he grabbed her by the waist and did a little dance.

"We can get married now, gal — married in church if you want to."

Ada was so overcome that she had to sit down and rest before she could take it all in. Married — after all this time. A house, a home for Molly, so that she could be like other bairns. God had remembered her at last. "And about time, too," she muttered, lifting her eyes to the ceiling.

Once the death certificates were obtained they began to make the wedding arrangements.

"I want it done proper like — in church," she informed him.

Rob had been leaning towards a register office ceremony but she wasn't having that. She'd served too long an apprenticeship to have second best when the real thing was due.

Mr. Brinner was asked to give her away and his wife and Lily to be witnesses.

"Who'll stand for you, and what about Molly?" she asked Rob.

"I reckon she ought to be bridesmaid. She'd love it, the little show-off," he laughed and though Ada wasn't quite sure about it, she agreed to let her go to the church and at least wear a pretty party dress.

Rob didn't know who to ask to be best man. He'd lost touch again with his lads and during the years had kept to himself. But the need was dispensed with when one Saturday morning, only a week or so before the wedding was due, a deputation of Ada's family arrived on the doorstep. Mrs. Brinner ran upstairs to tell Ada, who calmly told her to bring them up.

"If they start owt, I'll chuck them downstairs one by one," she laughed.

"We've heard you're getting wed and we want to give a hand." Bert was the spokesman.

"Well, you know what you can do with your hands," Ada snapped.

"Calm yourself down, Ada. We know damn well we haven't been all we should, but neither have you if you tell the truth."

"How did you get to know about the wedding, then?" she asked, sidetracking any apology they might have been expecting.

"Young Molly. She's been telling all town that she's going to be bridesmaid at her Mammy's wedding next Saturday."

Bert couldn't help laughing and Ada vainly tried to cover her smile. "I said we shouldn't have told her. You know what she's like, the little devil."

"Oh, shut up, Ada. We've come to make up, though with you, God knows how long it will last. I'd like to give you away."

Bert give her away — offering the olive branch — well, what next!

"You're too late. Old Brinner's giving me away," she snapped.

"Just a minute, Ada. Stop being so hoity-toity. If Bert's here to make amends then let him. Mr. Brinner can stand for me. Give in and don't be so pig-headed," Rob chimed in now, trying to avoid what looked like another row. They weren't half a funny lot, these Skiptons.

"Hummmmn — well — are you eating humble pie, our Bert?" she grinned cheekily.

"No, I aren't — no more than you, you silly bitch — but I've come to make up if you'll shut your mouth long enough to let me."

And it was so. Ada chose her outfit carefully, making sure she avoided brown. Lily's warning about that colour being unlucky for such occasions had proved right. Ada wasn't making the same mistake again. Instead she chose navy with blue accessories.

Molly would not rest until she was told that she could walk down the aisle behind her Mammy — and carry a small posy of flowers.

"I want to be a proper bridesmaid," she announced.

Ada wondered how she would feel when she was older and realised how things had been. She gave in because she knew full well that her daughter was more than capable of causing a right to-do if she was thwarted. Once they were married and had a house she really would have to take her in hand. She wasn't a bad lass, just a bit too old fashioned and big for her boots. Ada put it down to the situation she had been born into and no-one could blame the bairn for that. She had to do something to compensate. She'd come to no harm if she grew up with the same character she now showed. Any repercussions would be like water off a duck's back to Molly.

The wedding took place in St. John Street Methodist Church. As she walked up the street on Bert's arm and gazed at number 64 she almost broke down and cried. Such memories — a lifetime of sadness and sorrow.

"Come on, our Ada, don't take on. I feel a bit like you at the minute. But, by the hell, we had some good times and all, didn't we?" Bert — dear old Bert — trying to help with a few kind words.

"I'll say this for you, you look a right bobby dazzler. But then you always did, even when you had nowt. Ha'penny top and farthing tail — that's what I used to say. She'll not let anybody know when she's down, won't our Ada. She'll put on a show if the devil stands at her feet. Come on, give us a smile," he laughed as they reached the church door.

A small wedding tea was held at the Brinners in the front room. This was Mrs. Brinner's wedding present, and she had made the most welcome spread, complete with a tiny wedding cake — the third one Ada had cut. Maybe this would be the lucky one.

After the tea, Rob disappeared soon to return with his big brown portmanteau.

"Leaving already then?" said Ada. "By hek, that hasn't taken long." She looked up at him, puzzling out what he was up to now.

"Shut your blithering and get your coat on. We're going on holiday for a few days — a belated honeymoon."

"What with?" she asked, for the wedding had swallowed up quite a bit of money.

"Never you mind what with. I saved a bit from that lot we sent Kathleen," he told her and she smiled. He really was shaping up was our Rob.

Ada, Rob and Molly stayed at a guest house in the centre of York. Molly had gone along for neither of her parents could leave her for that length of time with anyone else.

It was clean and the food was good, and no-one knew other than that it was a little family break. On the Monday Rob insisted that they had a photograph taken, in one of these places where you returned two hours later to pick up the print. He ordered three copies.

"What the devil do you want all that lot for?" Ada laughed, and he told her to wait and see.

The rest and the break did them all good, and once back in Brid life took on a different meaning for Ada. She was legally now Mrs. Clamp — and Molly had been made legal now through the marriage too. And then she thought about the christening. She'd forgotten all about that with all the fuss. Better get that done next, and she'd ask Bert, Lizzie and Cissie to be godparents. That would settle their hash.

One night, with Molly tucked up in bed, Rob asked for the writing paper and envelopes. Ada watched as he laboriously wrote a letter and bending over his shoulder read aloud what he had put down.

"Dear Mother, I am sorry that I have not written before, but I have been very busy and a lot has gone on. You will find enclosed a picture of me with my wife and little girl. We had it taken on holiday last week. She is a good woman and you will like her I am sure. Just what you always said I needed. Molly my little girl is as bright as a

145

button and one day soon I shall bring them down to see you. That would be good for us all. Best love, Your everloving son, Rob."

The following Sunday under much protest Molly was christened. Ada, watching the little service taking place at the font, saw the look of pride on her family's faces as they became godparents to her daughter and felt, for the first time in many a year, a feeling of complete security and warmth.

As they came out of the church, Molly skipped to the front, hanging onto Bert's and Cissie's hand. By the hek, they didn't half spoil her now. Rob held Ada's arm and made her stand still in the aisle as he pressed a small packet into her hand.

"What's this then?" she asked. He told her to shut up and open the packet.

She did and out fell a small door key — the key to one of the new council houses, on the new estate. Tears rose and fell. She was laughing and crying and jibbering all at the same time.

Rob placed his hand over her lips to quieten her down. "All right then, missus?" he asked.

"A1 at Lloyds, my love," she smiled.

Home — home and dry — at last.